THE GIRL IN THE BACK ROW

THE GIRL IN THE BACK ROW

THE LAST VAMPIRE™ BOOK 2

JUDITH BERENS MARTHA CARR MICHAEL ANDERLE

First US edition, June 2019
Print ISBN: 978-1-64202-318-3

DEDICATIONS

From Martha

To everyone who still believes in magic
and all the possibilities that holds.
To all the readers who make this
entire ride so much fun.
And to my son, Louie and so many wonderful friends who
remind me all the time of what
really matters and how wonderful
life can be in any given moment.

From Michael

To Family, Friends and
Those Who Love
To Read.
May We All Enjoy Grace
To Live The Life We Are
Called.

CHAPTER ONE

"This is the most important weekend of the year, Vickie." Alexis yawned and stretched on her towel laying on the grass in their backyard. "Come Monday, this all goes away. School starts, and we lose our freedom for nine long months."

Vickie adjusted the sunglasses on her face and squirmed a little in the heat of the sun. Her pale skin dripped with sweat. Alexis had told her it was important to have at least a slight tan when they headed back to school, so she did her best to play along.

"Are we not allowed to do this during the school year? Can't we relax when we aren't in school?"

Alexis giggled. "Yeah, but it's different. The first day of school is officially the end of summer. You'll have some nights, but there will be homework, and the weather will cool off. We'll close the pool and stay inside all winter." She sighed and closed her eyes. "It won't be like this again. Not until next year, anyway. Relax while you can."

But as Vickie lay on her towel, she couldn't relax. Her

face grimaced, and her stomach tightened. *I don't feel right. Something bad is happening.*

Without saying a word, she stood and wandered to the front of the house.

"Vickie?" Alexis rolled over and opened her eyes to see her friend gone. "Hey, where'd you go?"

In the front yard, she scanned the area, her vampire powers on high alert as she sensed something that left her wary and uneasy.

She walked down the driveway and reached the street. Vickie looked toward the intersection on one end and saw nothing. She spun to look in the other direction.

"Vickie! What's the deal?" Her friend walked swiftly to catch up with her.

The vampire glanced at a small boy who did his best to bounce a basketball on the sidewalk. The ball hit an uneven section and dribbled into the middle of the road.

Without thinking, the child walked out to retrieve it. A careless driver barreled down the road, glancing at the GPS on his phone.

Alexis saw what was unfolding and covered her mouth in horror. Vickie gritted her teeth, tapped into her vampire speed, and rocketed forward to rescue the child.

In the blink of an eye, she reached the tow-headed boy, grasped him firmly, and spun toward the sidewalk. Despite her speed, however, it was too late.

She felt the presence of the two tons of shiny blue metal without even looking back. Instinctively, she shielded the boy, wrapped her arms around him, and turned her back to the car.

The tires squealed as her sunglasses slipped off her face

and arced to bounce off the windshield. The man screeched to a halt in the center of the road, his mouth open and his eyes wide in amazement.

Vickie knelt in front of the boy to make sure he was okay. He was speechless and could only nod at her.

The driver scrambled out of the car and looked in both directions. "Did anyone else see that?"

Uh oh. Alexis ran barefoot down the sidewalk to see if she could somehow ease the situation or encourage his confusion. He obviously couldn't believe what he'd seen, so she could use that, hopefully. "See what?"

"That… I…" The man put his hands on his hips, unable to explain despite the dent in his fender.

"I saw you speed down the road and almost run over this poor boy," Vickie accused him hotly.

"Yeah, but—" He placed his hand on the back of his head and stared at Vickie who showed no signs of injury, then back at his car's fender.

"He's fine now, you can go." The vampire waved him off. Some of her four-hundred-year-old habits still existed. She wasn't used to repeating herself or dealing with fools.

He walked away, muttering, "I don't know how I'll explain this one to the wife." His face twisted in bewilderment as he cast furtive and possibly even suspicious looks at both girls.

Meanwhile, the boy sat beside his basketball. "That was cool," he whispered and gazed at Vickie in awe. She put her hand on his shoulder and winked at him. "You're okay now. But don't tell anyone."

He smiled and nodded in response. "My dad breaks stuff all the time and tells me not to tell Mom."

She winced but Alexis exhaled a small laugh. "Yeah, just like that. And stay out of the road," she ordered him. He nodded, picked up his basketball, and ran down the street toward his house.

"Boy, that is some bad parenting for another day," Alexis said and watched the child until he reached his front sidewalk.

Vickie smiled proudly. "I had a feeling something was wrong."

Her friend gave her a sidelong glance as she turned to walk back to the house. "Right, but you really can't do that."

"Would you rather I let the poor boy be hit by the car?"

"No…no, never. But…there has to be a better way to handle this. You'll out yourself by accident before you know it."

"Even if that boy tells his mom that a super-girl with amazing speed rescued him, she won't believe a word he says." Vickie laughed as they reached the towels in the backyard.

Alexis stretched out again with another sigh. "I know. You got lucky this time. This time."

***

Vickie stood in front of the entrance to Clear Lake High School as dozens of students breezed past her.

Her hands gripped the straps of her backpack and dragged them to meet in the middle of her chest while her fingers interlocked.

Close to her left shoulder, Alexis smiled.

"Are you ready for this?" she asked.

"I don't know," the vampire replied nervously.

The last two months had been a whirlwind. Alexis gave Vickie a crash course on America but spent less time with her than they had in Austria.

The teenager wanted a little time to herself in order to enjoy her friends and the last of the summer. For every afternoon spent walking through the neighborhood describing the average American family—"You mean everyone owns a car here?"—there were multiple evenings when Alexis left Vickie at the house while she caught a movie or went for ice cream with her friends.

At the time, the vampire understood. Having to constantly explain American culture must have been exhausting for her friend, and she showed remarkable patience while doing it.

However, standing in front of the school, she couldn't help but feel unprepared.

Alexis could sense her adopted sister's nerves. Although they weren't united by blood, the two of them had developed a close connection.

"You'll do great," she assured her. "Nothing prepares you for high school. You simply have to go in and be a part of it."

"Were you nervous on your first day?" Vickie asked without taking her eyes off the massive school building ahead of her.

"Oh yeah." Alexis laughed, stepped forward, and turned to catch her gaze. "But I was also a freshman. Freshmen are like...blood in the water to a group of sharks. They're easy targets. But you're not coming in as a freshman. You're a sophomore so it's different. They won't come after you."

"Who's 'they?'" Vickie asked, concerned. "Do I need to keep my defenses up?"

"Relax, this isn't the Thirty Years' War in there. It's only high school," she told her. "Come on. We'll go in, find your locker, and get you into homeroom."

They walked up the sidewalk. On either side of them, students laid across the metal benches to soak in the sunlight. A few of them puffed on cigarette butts. On the grass behind the benches, three boys kicked a hacky sack between them.

For these kids, the ensuing minutes were the last remnants of summer vacation. Once that bell sounded throughout the halls, they would become slaves to the school schedule for nine months.

They were in no rush to get started.

As the girls entered the school building, Vickie marveled at how different the atmosphere was from her placement testing day.

The hustle and bustle of the new school year seemed to bounce off the walls. Every two or three seconds, another locker slammed.

In the main hall, a group of boys joked around, pushing and shoving each other, and laughed about their summer escapades. A few of their buddies sprawled on the hard tile floor, their backpacks used as makeshift pillows that were about as comfortable as they looked.

Various groups of friends wore the easy, relieved smiles of reunion. Maybe they weren't looking forward to spending all day shuttling from classroom to classroom, but at least they would go through it with their closest pals.

"Your locker is right next to your homeroom," Alexis

explained and led her down the main stairwell. "You're in the English Hall."

At the bottom of the steps, they turned left. Vickie's eyes widened as she looked down the long corridor on the way to her locker. She had never seen so many people crammed into one location in her life.

It almost felt like Summerfest, except nobody was drunk. There were tall kids, short kids, beautiful kids, and homely kids. Some had clearly gotten up early to make sure their hair and makeup were on point. Others looked like they rolled out of bed and walked directly into school.

About halfway down the hall, they reached a line of blue lockers opposite a side exit door and stairwell.

"Here you go—number 1180," Alexis announced and pointed to one of the lockers in the middle. "Go ahead. I showed you how to work the lock."

Vickie nodded and walked confidently to the locker and spun the combination dial until she could raise the handle and open the tall, narrow storage space.

Alexis smiled and looked over her shoulder. "This is your home for the next three years," she said. "Everything you want to bring to school will probably go in here. Anything you want to keep safe goes in here. This is the place."

With that much buildup, Vickie expected to be impressed but honestly, it was nondescript. A few hooks jutted out from the sides and a metal shelf sat above them. The rest of it was empty.

"It doesn't look like much," she said.

Alexis tapped her on the shoulder and pointed to another girl several lockers down. "Your locker is what you make of it," she said. The girl was taping up several photos of her boyfriend on the inside of her door. "That's your job. But don't worry about that yet. On the list of things you need to spend your time on, locker decoration is something that can be done anytime."

Vickie dropped her backpack to the floor, hunched down, and unzipped it. She pulled out a few notebooks and tossed them onto the shelf at the top of her locker. Alexis had told her that she didn't need to bring everything with her everywhere she went, and she was to use her locker to swap out supplies between classes.

"There you go," her sister said. "Now, what's the first thing in the school day?"

"Homeroom," Vickie answered.

"That's right. And the door is right there. Nice and easy."

Vickie looked at the door of the homeroom, then back at Alexis. "So this is it, then?" she asked. "You have to go to your homeroom?"

Alexis nodded as a loud bell rang through the hallway. "That's the first bell," she said. "I have to drop a few things in my locker near the library, then I'll be in my homeroom. But look at me—you'll do great. All you have to worry about on the first day of school is making it to your classes on time and being in the right room. And we've gone over the layout of this place. You know where everything is, and you have your schedule. You got this."

She patted her on the shoulder and crossed the hallway traffic to skip up the stairs, leaving Vickie alone in front of her homeroom door. A few other kids slid past her to enter the room, and she took a deep breath.

You're in high school now, Victoria. Let's do this.

The vampire walked into the room and smiled. All the pictures on the wall and the words written on the chalkboard were in the German language.

As luck would have it, she was assigned the homeroom of one of the school's German teachers, Mr. Gunther Thoms.

He was a man full of character. With a German accent almost as thick as his barrel chest, he was not only a native German but an accomplished Tae Kwon Do enthusiast.

Although he was around five feet tall, he bore the well-earned reputation of someone who could rip you in half several times before you hit the ground.

Despite those credentials, Mr. Thoms was a sweet man, ready with a smile. Every day, he sat behind his desk wearing a Clear Lake High School Tennis Team polo shirt tucked into a pair of pleated slacks—he was also the school's tennis coach.

His dark-gray hair was combed over and across his balding head, which looked natural when he stood. When he looked down at the paperwork on his desk, however, it always revealed his follicular shortcomings.

Still, given the man's fighting ability, nobody bothered to joke about it.

Vickie watched as her other classmates sat in rows in the room—four rows, to be exact. There appeared to be some kind of organization there, but she didn't know what it was.

She chose a seat a desk up against the left wall of the classroom and tried her best to blend in and look natural.

Once everyone was in the room, the second bell rang and one of the older kids shut the door.

"Okay, is everybody here?" Mr. Thoms asked. "Okay. First, we do announcements. Then, we do introductions. Mr. Babbitt, go ahead with announcements."

A very tall blond boy in a baggy sweatshirt stood and grabbed the pink sheet of paper from the teacher's desk. He crossed briskly to the podium in front of the classroom and read the school news of the day aloud.

Given that it was the first day of the school year, there wasn't much substance to the announcements other than a few words to welcome the kids to another year of school. The youth who delivered the announcements made very little effort to hide his boredom at having to read general greetings and updates about the sporting events that would be held that upcoming weekend.

Once he was done, he tossed the sheet of paper onto Mr. Thoms' desk and returned to his chair.

"Okay, okay," the man boomed. "Time to meet the freshmen. When it's your turn, you stand, say your name, and tell us something about you. Okay? Okay, go."

At the front of the row in which Vickie sat, a boy stood and, his voice shaking, muttered his name and something about himself. She didn't pay close attention.

Next, the girl sitting directly in front of her stood and did the same. But this time, the vampire was completely distracted.

I think I'm in the wrong row.

Once the girl sat, all eyes were on her. She stood and said sheepishly, "My name is Vickie, and I'm actually a sophomore, so I'm in the wrong row."

The students laughed and she slunk over to the next row where she sat in the back while some of her classmates shook their heads.

After the introductions, the freshmen sat in nervous silence. The few kids in her row talked among themselves. A boy and a girl seemed friendly with one another—a skinny, dark-haired boy with a hooked nose and baggy jeans and a scowling, unpleasant-looking girl with short brown hair whose face lit up when she smiled. Sadly, though, she didn't smile much at all.

In the fourth row, the baggy sweatshirt-wearing boy walked up to Mr. Thoms, who jotted notes at his desk.

"All right, Mr. Thoms. First day of school. You know what time it is," he announced with a devilish smile.

Mr. Thoms sighed. "Okay, okay," he said. "You are the victim, yes?"

The boy gave him a thumbs-up and jogged over to his backpack, from which he produced a white-powdered doughnut.

"Do you need to stretch first?" he asked.

Mr. Thoms pushed himself up from his chair and threw his leg up a few times to loosen his muscles. "I'm getting old." He chuckled wryly. "I don't want to hurt myself."

Vickie glanced around the room in confusion. The row of freshmen seemed to have the same expression as her, but the other kids smiled knowingly.

The boy and the teacher squared up to each other. It seemed a little unfair as the boy stood more than a foot taller than the man. The student stuck the doughnut between his teeth and craned his neck forward.

In one fluid motion, the pudgy German man kicked his

foot straight up and knocked the doughnut out of his mouth. Powdered sugar puffed into a cloud in its wake.

The room erupted in cheers. Vickie laughed, although she honestly didn't understand the entertainment value of it.

"Okay, okay," the teacher said, "no more show. Get ready for class coming up." He waddled back to the desk and sat once again. The kids all relived the experience while he simply chuckled.

Are all classes like this? Do all teachers know the art of combat?

Before she could ponder these thoughts any further, the bell rang, and everyone stood from their desks.

It was time for her first class.

CHAPTER TWO

D*on't be late.*

Those words echoed in Vickie's head as she walked out of homeroom. It was her first day of school and being late would draw a lot of unwanted attention her way. Now that she had already embarrassed herself once, she was determined to not let that happen again.

She only had a few minutes to get to the other side of the school. Her algebra class with Mr. Gilbert was in the Math Hall—a new section added to the school within the last five years.

Her first reaction when she stepped out into the hallway was the temptation to tap into her powers and speed through the crowd.

When she had a burst of energy like that, her senses were so strong that she could instantly see the pockets of space between people in a crowd. It would be simple, and she would likely be the first person in class.

However, with so many people watching, there was no way she could do that. If being late would draw unwanted awareness, disappearing in a blur in front of all the students likely to witness it would result in far more attention than she would ever ask for.

Vickie chose to go up the stairs across from her locker, which were fairly uncrowded. She skipped every other step but tried to move as fast as humanly possible.

The floor above hers was the Philosophy and Social Studies Hall, and like the English Hall, it was packed with students.

"Sorry," she muttered to someone as she accidentally rammed into them when she turned the corner. The student shot her a dirty look.

Carefully, she slipped past people one by one and tried to move through the crowd without colliding with anyone.

Why does everyone move so slowly? Don't they want to be on time, too? They'll be late and everyone will know.

The hallway opened into the main lobby, where the stuffiness of the tight quarters in the corridor relaxed into a refreshing atmosphere as people spread out.

This is where I make up for lost time, Vickie thought when she saw the open path in front of her.

At first, she ran and took the gaps as quickly as she could. But after a moment, she looked around and studied her surroundings and realized nobody else was sprinting.

Don't draw attention to yourself, she reminded herself.

She slowed a little and now power-walked across the lobby until she reached the History Hall on the other side of the building. The Math Hall extended out from the end of that one, so she was almost there.

Of course, reaching a new corridor meant the traffic

funneled back into a crawl, and the sudden slowdown forced her to again bump into her fellow students.

"Sorry," she said and earned more annoyed looks.

Her feet seemed to bounce a little from her irritation while she moved anxiously through the crowd. To her surprise, some students milled about aimlessly with not a care in the world. Some even stood beside their lockers.

A boy hit on one of his classmates at one locker. Two buddies looked over their phones at another.

None of them seemed very concerned about getting to class.

Vickie reached the end of the History Hall and turned right into the newer wing of the school. Finally, the Math Hall.

Once she reached her classroom, she bolted in to discover that only two other students were sitting there.

It must be a small class.

In the front corner of the room, an older, overweight man with white hair and thick black-framed glasses sat with his arms folded and stared out over the sea of desks.

"Excuse me," she said to the man, "is there a particular row I need to sit in?"

He shook his head and pushed on the bridge of his glasses to reposition them on his nose. "Sit wherever you like. I'll rearrange you when everyone's here."

Vickie nodded and took a seat near the back of the room, hoping to blend in as much as possible.

For another full minute, she sat in silence and wondered where all the other kids were. She shifted a little uncomfortably in her seat—being only one of three students made her feel like she stood out—and heaved an inward sigh of relief when a wave of students poured through the door and hastily selected desks. More than two dozen kids entered and the last one made it into the room as the bell sounded.

"All right, all right," the man in front shouted. "Grab a seat. I'll take attendance in alphabetical order by your last name, and I will point to the desk you should sit in."

He stood and walked to the front of the room with a notebook at the ready. One by one, he walked up and down the rows, announcing names and seating assignments. To Vickie's horror, her desk was in the middle of the front row.

Several minutes passed as the teacher assigned desks and took attendance, then he walked slowly to the front of the class and stood directly before Vickie.

He grabbed the waist of his pants and tugged on them to straighten the brown slacks that had to be at least twenty years old. The buttons on his short-sleeved white dress shirt strained to stay closed over his gut. His brown tie stopped well short of the bottom of his belly and rested comfortably atop the shelf it provided.

"My name is Mr. Gilbert," he said, "and this is Algebra Two. These desks will be your assigned seats for the rest of this semester, so get comfortable."

Great.

"Because there are some new faces here, I would like you each to stand and provide an interesting detail when you introduce yourself to the class."

He shuffled his feet to his desk and squeezed himself back into the chair and folded his arms on top of his stomach.

Each student stood and shared little anecdotes about childhood injuries, favorite TV shows, and celebrity encounters.

Next, it was Vickie's turn. Her mind had raced in an effort to come up with an appropriate factoid about herself.

"Hi, I'm Vickie, and I cannot be killed unless you cut my head off."

"Hi, I'm Vickie, and I was put to sleep in the seventeenth century and slept for four hundred years."

"Hi, I'm Vickie, and I have the strength of ten bodybuilders."

She shook all those off and stood to introduce herself.

"Hi, my name is Vickie Hewitt, and I just moved here from Austria."

"Really?" Mr. Gilbert asked and raised his eyebrows in interest for the first time in this exercise. "When did you move here?"

"Yes, sir," she replied. "In July."

"Well, welcome to America," he said excitedly.

Vickie appreciated the friendliness. He was the first person in the entire school to welcome her like that.

She sat again and a chill ran up her spine from the cold, hard plastic desk. In her homeroom, the chairs were softer. She could rock back and forth in her seat and the room was much, much warmer.

On that September day, Milwaukee experienced one of its trademark late-summer heat waves. The temperature outside was over eighty degrees, and the humidity was off the charts.

Inside the air-conditioned school, the temperature varied with each room. The older, more established wings of the school—such as the one that held the English Hall—were sweltering, thanks to an inefficient cooling system in the older structures.

The newer wings like the Math Hall were *very* efficient. In fact, they were too efficient. Because the thermostat had to be kept low to keep the older halls at a temperature everyone could endure, the newer halls became like refrigerators. Students joked that they could see their breath in these halls during the hot summer weather.

The temperature wasn't the only thing that bothered Vickie about the desk. The overall comfort level of it wasn't much better. The hard plastic and the affixed desktop offered nothing in the way of adjustment, so many students had to contort their bodies simply to be able to take notes or get comfortable at all.

She tried to push her irritation aside when Mr. Gilbert began teaching and introduced the students to the basic concepts of algebra they would need to review before they could move on to more advanced lessons.

As the teacher wrote different simple equations on the whiteboard, Vickie's mind began to wander.

Why are we learning these things if we are expected to already know them? Shouldn't we be in this class to learn new things? How long will he spend teaching us the lessons from Algebra One?

But when she looked around the room, several of her students were taking studious notes. Others were falling asleep, their heads bobbing up and down.

But nobody questioned the teacher.

Finally, Vickie raised her hand like Alexis had taught her to do when she had a question.

"A question?" the teacher asked and pointed to her.

"Yes," she replied, "why are you teaching this?"

The air seemed to be sucked out of the room. The tension was palpable—enough so that she looked around to see what the big deal was.

"Excuse me?" Mr. Gilbert asked, puzzled. "This is algebra, and this is Algebra Two."

"I know that," she said, "and I don't mean to be disrespectful. I simply mean...we learned this already, right? This is only review."

The teacher nodded. "Yes, but review is important after a long summer vacation. Class, how many of you remember this stuff forward and backward? A show of hands?"

Around the room, two other students raised their hands besides Vickie. The rest met the question with blank stares.

"I appreciate your concern," the teacher told Vickie. "But normally, we start with a review because students tend to forget these concepts after a long school break."

"Suck up," the boy behind her whispered under his breath. Vickie didn't understand what he meant by that phrase.

But she wasn't stupid. She could tell the class was not impressed with her question. A few of them gave her dirty looks. She shrugged awkwardly, uncertain how to respond to a situation like this.

Given the responses around her, she had done enough, so she simply slouched in the seat and tried to stay as invisible as possible for the rest of the class. The subject matter was as boring to her as it was to everyone else.

But it wasn't because it was algebra and she was a teenager. It was because she knew all this stuff already and didn't need to re-learn it.

I sure hope we don't constantly go over the same stuff in all my classes.

The other thing that caught her attention was the amount of goofing off going on.

Mr. Gilbert was far from a captivating teacher. He also had little desire to call on students to participate. He preferred to give lectures, and the students could ask questions if they wanted.

As a result, most students mentally checked out of the class about fifteen minutes in, and they still had more than twenty-five minutes to go in the period.

Some texted each other, although cell phones were prohibited in classrooms. Others doodled in their notebooks while a few students slept the period away.

All this behavior confused Vickie.

Why go to school if you won't engage with it? What's the point of spending all this time and money here? They're not learning anything, and they admitted to needing to learn this stuff.

Vickie observed this with dumbfounded awe until the period finally ended and the bell ended her frustration.

Her instinct was to bolt from her desk and sprint out of the room to get to her next class. As difficult as it was, she fought the urge after she'd watched everyone get up.

Normal students appear to not be in much of a hurry to get to their next class. I have to remember that. Slow down and don't stand out. Take your time getting to class and you'll blend in a little more.

CHAPTER THREE

Vickie fought every urge to sprint across the halls. *You've already drawn too much attention to yourself. Fit in. Pace yourself. Nobody else is late. You won't be either.*

On the far end of the Math Hall, three girls leaned against the row of blue lockers. The one in the middle kept one foot off the floor and rested it on the lockers behind her. She chewed casually on a piece of bubble gum and occasionally popped it with an unimpressed look on her face.

She was short and blonde, with tight jeans and a red spaghetti-strap top covered by a thin white cardigan. On each side of her stood two tall brunettes. The trio giggled amongst themselves while they enjoyed the view of the other kids rushing down the halls.

"Another year." The blonde girl sighed. "Look at Molly over there. I see she didn't discover shampoo over summer vacation." Her friends laughed. "Like, seriously? How hard is it to wash your hair and run a comb through it? She looks like such a greaseball."

The blonde looked at her perfectly painted fingernails that featured bright red polish. "It's like some of these people don't even realize they are out in public. Have a little pride in yourselves."

Meanwhile, Vickie moved through the halls while anxiety bubbled constantly under her skin. *Am I moving fast enough? Or too fast? Is anyone looking at me?* She scanned the immediate area and checked the gazes of the other kids. *It doesn't seem like anyone is paying attention. Maybe I'm fitting in. Wait, is that guy looking at me over there? No, maybe not. Those girls are, though. Is it the way I'm walking?*

As she hustled past, the blonde scoffed. "I hear the new girl is from Germany or something. Whatever. Look at her run. What a dork." Vickie came within earshot as the girl muttered under her breath. "*Lauf, kleines Mädchen. Du willst nicht zu spät kommen.*"

Vickie stopped to look at the blonde. Her hearing had picked up every word.

"Excuse me, who are you calling 'little girl?'" She walked directly to the trio, who arched their eyebrows in disbelief that they were even approached.

"I didn't call you anything. Don't flatter yourself."

"I heard what you said. Don't talk to me that way."

The blonde pushed lazily away from the locker as Vickie stepped forward. "I'll talk to you however I want. You're new here. Learn to pay a little respect."

The vampire shook her head. "I was raised to respect everyone. But you clearly don't deserve it."

"Excuse me?"

The hair on the back of her neck stood up and sent a quick chill down her spine. She slid her tongue along the top row of teeth and felt her fangs beginning to poke out. *Don't draw attention to them. You need to get out of here.*

Before anything else could happen, Alexis appeared seemingly out of nowhere, hooked her arm in Vickie's, and dragged her away.

"Go back to Germany," the blonde shouted and her friends laughed.

The vampire stumbled awkwardly, caught off-guard by the sudden appearance of her new sister. She caught her footing and adjusted her stride to walk alongside her. "What was that for?"

Alexis released her arm. "That's Megan Fitz. She's the biggest jerk in the entire school. I knew she was simply trying to make you angry."

"Why does she want me angry?"

"It's what she does." Alexis rolled her eyes. "She likes to embarrass other people. It makes her feel good."

Vickie frowned as she considered this. "That's a strange thing to do to make yourself feel good."

"Welcome to high school. I'm surprised she didn't try to trip you. That's how she got me back in freshman year. A week before Christmas break, she saw me running down the hall to make it to my physical science exam. She stuck her foot out and tripped me so I actually fell hard."

"Were there a lot of people around?"

"Oh, tons. See, I was moving so fast that I didn't only hit the floor—I went airborne and landed on my face. I almost broke my nose, and I got a huge bruise on my cheek. The pictures from Christmas that year are hard for me to look at. I had to wear so much makeup simply to cover everything up."

Vickie's jaw dropped. "And nobody did anything about it?"

"This is high school, Vickie. Everyone looks out for themselves here. What would anybody do? We all went about our day. I was late for the exam, too."

"I would have charged up to her and crushed her windpipe." Vickie balled her fists for emphasis.

"Yeah. See, that's the kind of thing people frown on here. Tripping somebody is a prank. What you're talking about is straight-up murdering someone."

As they walked, Alexis thought of that holiday. There was another reason why pictures from that year made her sad. It was also the last Christmas before her mom was diagnosed with cancer.

The last Christmas things could still be called normal.

I would gladly go back to that Christmas. Any day. I don't care about my face.

"I still feel like I should do something about her." Vickie turned to look at Megan in the distance, who only now started to make her way down the hall to her next class.

"What did she do to you?"

There was a brief pause. "Nothing, I guess. She was condescending to me."

Alexis laughed. "Well, you'll need more than 'condescending' to argue for retaliation. We all should be so lucky."

"So she gets away with being a jerk, then."

Alexis' mind drifted back to that Christmas when she'd sat on her bed with her face in her hands and sobbed. Whenever she'd looked in the mirror, she thought of how everything would be ruined. Her favorite time of the year and she had a massive purple bruise covering the side of her face. No matter how much makeup she caked on, she could still see it.

Her mom had walked into the room, sat down beside her, and put her arm around her. "Alexis, no one will even notice." She rubbed her shoulder. "The only reason you see it right now is because you know it's there and you're looking for it."

Alexis sniffled. "She ruined my Christmas. Now, all I can think about is how awful I look. I had a great new dress picked out. I was so excited to party with my cousins. And now this."

Her mom shook her head. "What are you afraid of? What makes you so scared to go out in public looking like that?"

"I just… I look stupid!"

"Honey, you have a bruise on your cheek. No one will assume you did that on purpose. Even though you can barely see it, it's no big deal. They'll probably feel sorry for you more than anything."

Then, her mom gave her some advice that she would carry with her for the rest of her life. "Don't let anyone else hold that much power over your happiness."

When she finished telling that story to Vickie, the vampire smiled. "You took that to heart? That's good advice."

Alexis tilted her head from one side to the other. "I'd like to say I never worried about what someone else thought of me ever again, but that's not true. I'm still a high school girl. But it was good advice. I figured I should pass it on to you, too."

"Your mother was very smart."

"Yes. Yes, she was. Some days, I really wish she could be here to help me walk through all this."

Vickie understood but she couldn't shake the feeling that this Megan girl would be a thorn in her side. "I don't know why Megan would pick on me, then."

"Because you're the new girl. Fresh blood. She's spent the last couple of years torturing the rest of us. You're a new victim to torment."

"How do I get her to stop?"

Alexis pursed her lips and thought of her mom once more. "My mom said that bullies will lay off if you don't react to what they say or do. Don't give them the satisfaction. But I never found that to be true. I guess the best thing you can do is ignore her and wait it out until graduation. I don't know. She still bothers me, too."

When Vickie arrived at her next class, she walked into the room and chose a spot in the back again. Minutes later, the bell rang as the last few students poured through the door. One of them was Megan Fitz.

She took a seat beside Vickie and glared at her. "If it isn't the little girl."

"Stop calling me that." She sneered at her.

"I'll call you whatever I want. You don't get to tell me what to do."

The vampire bit her tongue and did her best to keep her cool. She would now be stuck with Megan in this class every day for a semester. She decided the best thing she could do was keep her mouth shut for now.

The opportunity to get back at her would come, just not at that moment.

CHAPTER FOUR

Hannes jogged down the narrow brick-paved street and glanced at his watch. *I'm late. If I run in there while they're in the middle of a prayer, I'll be in major trouble.*

The long black cloth billowed in his arms as he clutched it. The wind had picked up, and rain clouds formed overhead. Looking unkempt was almost as bad as showing up late, so he picked up the pace as he ran.

It was another gloomy day in Salzburg. While most people would complain about cloudy weather, it was the perfect atmosphere for him and the group he was about to meet with. They always felt a cloudy, gray day added great ambiance to their monthly meetings.

He stopped at the front steps of the Dom zu Salzburg. Its dual spires soared high into the sky and appeared to poke at the rain clouds that threatened a downpour.

Hannes pulled open the front door of the massive cathedral and scuttled in as a few raindrops sprinkled onto the top of his salt-and-pepper hair. *Just made it.*

The inside of the cathedral was almost pitch black.

Candlelight barely illuminated the chapel where worshippers sat scattered in the pews to pray quietly.

After one deep breath, he turned to the stairway that led down to the crypt. He spared a glance around to make sure no one was watching as he sidestepped the *CRYPT CLOSED* sign.

It often closed for worship services and other gatherings, so it was not out of the ordinary to see it unavailable to the public. This made the Dom zu Salzburg a great meeting place.

After he walked halfway down the stairway, he remembered the cloth in his arms. Hannes shook it open and pulled it over his head. The black robe covered his entire body. He pulled the hood over the top of his head, tilted his chin down, and continued his descent.

At the bottom of the stairs, the orange firelight permeated the space and a long row of candles lined one wall. Seated in front of it was a group of several dozen nondescript people dressed exactly like him.

Very few of those gathered knew each other's identities. Unless explicit and exceptional circumstances dictated otherwise, there was no need. They maintained their strict secrecy to protect themselves from public attention.

With his chin tucked so the hood would cover the top of his face, Hannes entered the crowd that huddled around a small blazing torch in the center of the circle they formed around it.

"This gathering of the Slayer Circle shall now commence. May God be with us all this evening," a man announced, and his deep voice resonated in the space.

He picked the torch up but kept his hood in place to

shadow his features. The light of the flames danced in the reflection on his glasses that peeked out from the black fabric. He went by the name of Gabriel, but it was understood that it was an alias used for convenience among the members of the Circle. "I would like to welcome all you children to this holiest of gatherings."

The Slayer Circle met in the darkness of the cathedral crypt. It was a time of quiet worship and remembrance of their ancestors—those who had worked tirelessly to rid the world of the vampire race and keep the Earth pure.

"Each one of us is a descendant from the original Circle." A murmur went up among the crowd and Gabriel raised his hand to silence them. "I know. We keep each other's anonymity and have stayed away from family gatherings all these years. I don't need to remind any of you of the story of our origins." He closed his eyes tightly and swallowed hard. "It was a dark time for the human race when we needed to be protected from the supernatural forces of the vampire race.

"Since then, generation after generation has left a clause in their will that in order to inherit, each succeeding member of the original families must gather together and remember." He raised the torch over his head to cast a long shadow onto the stone floor. "On this evening, we fulfill that promise once again and celebrate the anniversary of the Sang Crusade. On this day, hundreds of years ago, brave men and women set out on a tireless mission ordained by the righteous. They successfully struck down the bloodsucking menace."

His voice rose with the passion of fire and brimstone. "Brothers and sisters, we will not allow the memory of those who came before us to go quietly into the night. We preserve this day as a time of remembrance and reflection, for we were delivered from the depths of hell on Earth thanks to the sacrifices they made for us."

Gabriel lowered the torch and his silhouette shifted to the ceiling. "Tonight, we walk in quiet reverence of those brave souls. We read the stories they passed on to us and let the spirit flow within us. Also, we open the sacred texts of the Slayer Circle to experience the holy crusade waged on the vampire race once again. Their efforts were not in vain. They are always in our hearts, and we live our lives without fear."

He stopped speaking as a wrinkled, trembling hand raised from the back of the circle.

An old man stepped forward, his hand still raised as he pushed his way through the crowd. Once he reached the front, he pulled his hood off to reveal an ancient face, his skin sagging from his cheekbones.

"My friend," Gabriel said, "you do not protect your identity this night? Why do you break from the tradition of the Slayer Circle? You put your life at grave risk."

The man looked as though he had seen a ghost. His face was pale with fear, and he continued to tremble. "As I stand before you this night, I am troubled by a presence felt deep within my heart."

The leader scanned the room. Nobody raised their heads. "What do you feel, sir? Tonight is a night of reverent celebration of the peace our forefathers have bestowed upon us."

"This peace no longer exists." The old man's eyes

widened. "I fear for our souls. A presence has emerged upon the world once more."

A murmur rippled through the crowd of people.

"Silence, all of you." He leaned toward the man. "What presence do you speak of?"

"Vampires."

Even more hushed commotion stirred the group while Gabriel attempted to quiet them again.

"My elder, please explain yourself. Why do you feel a vampire presence exists in the world?"

His jaw shook as he spoke like he was cold, although he stood bare inches from the flame of the torch. "Several weeks ago, I lay in bed when a man in a black robe entered my bedroom. I leapt to my feet, hoping to either get away from him or defend myself from him. I wasn't sure which. He identified himself as Jannik."

Another murmur surged and Gabriel squinted one eye. Jannik had been one of the leaders of the Sang Crusade. He was a large, strong man who struck down more vampires than anyone else during that span of time.

"He was so tall. His shoulders were broad, and his hands were the size of baseball mitts. I marveled at how large he was, and yet I did not awake as he walked in. I didn't hear him coming. He merely stood there, motionless, and stared at me. Jannik instructed me to come to you and tell you that the Sang Crusade was a failure. They did not succeed in destroying the vampire race."

"That is impossible." The leader scoffed openly at the idea. "We have lived vampire-free for centuries."

"No, you haven't. Jannik says they have been in hiding.

There is a girl who recently awoke. She is in the world somewhere and she carries the vampire race with her."

"Does she pose a threat?"

"She is not dormant. Jannik simply said she is a vampire and she somehow escaped the Sang Crusade."

This was too much for Gabriel to process. For years, he had led the Slayer Circle in celebrations and appreciation for their deliverance from the vampire race. Now he was told that the vampires could potentially still pose a threat?

"I do not believe you. This must be your imagination or a dream you had. The vampires are no more."

The old man grabbed him by the robe and yanked him forward to stare desperately into his eyes. "It was not a dream. Jannik came to me. She is out there somewhere. The vampire race survives."

Several other members of the Circle hurried forward and pulled the old man off Gabriel.

"Please take him away," he ordered. "Remove him from the Circle." He adjusted his robe and straightened it as two men dragged the aged nuisance from the crypt.

The ancient screamed and shouted the entire way out. "You must listen to me. There is still a survivor. The vampire race was not extinguished. It still burns."

Gabriel shook his head with obvious disappointment. "I apologize for the disturbance on this, the holiest of evenings. That man must have been a long-time member of the Circle. It's very possible that his eyes deceived him and that he simply imagined the presence of Jannik. Has anyone else been visited by the presence of our illustrious forebear?"

Nobody raised their hands.

"That's what I thought. Now, come, let us join in appreciation for our forefathers."

The group chanted and sang that evening, watched over by the torches and the candles. They walked in circles and continued in the traditions they had kept alive for more than four hundred years.

But for the first time since he'd been called to lead their rituals, Gabriel's mind drifted. He worried that the old man might somehow be right. Was there really a surviving vampire in the world? And if there were, how would they go about finding her and removing her from existence?

As his brain thought of this, another fear gripped his consciousness. *What if we are too late? What if she has already feasted on the blood of humans? Did the Slayer Circle really not finish the work they started four hundred years ago? And would we be able to finish it before the vampire race once again takes over the world?*

At the end of the ceremony, everyone gathered to hear him speak once again. "Tonight, as you go on your way on this rainy night, do not fear the existence of vampires. Pay no mind to the accusations of a man who is unwell in the head. Instead, celebrate your safety. Celebrate the preservation of the human race. And celebrate the purity of the world in which we live—a world once held by vampires that no longer lives under that shadow."

The robed figures filed out while he stared at the torch in his hand. He sighed and shook his head. *What if the old man is right? How can we be sure?*

CHAPTER FIVE

For Vickie, the next few days were a blur. Her first full week in high school had overwhelmed her with new experiences. Growing up in a small town, she had never seen so many people in her life, much less in one place.

And being forced to interact with them on her own, away from Alexis for large chunks of the day, proved to be a stressful challenge to her.

It was now the first Friday evening of the school year. Alexis was excited as she walked through the house. "I can't wait to go out. This is the best part of school right here."

Vickie, who sat on the couch, shrugged. "What is the big deal about going out? We went out all summer."

"This is different. When you go out in the summer, you're simply together. You're bored during the day, so you get together at night. But during the school year, going out on Friday night is your big break. It's the time when you can unwind from all the stress and homework of the school week. It's…well, it's satisfying."

Her father smiled as he put his tablet down and leaned

back in his recliner with his feet up. "Where are you girls headed tonight?"

"Where else, Dad?"

He nodded knowingly. Johnny V's was the classic hangout for kids who went to Clear Lake High School. Located down the road from the school, the small diner was usually packed with kids who wanted a place to go but were too young to venture to the bars. They could order from a wide range of diner foods, sit at a booth or table big enough to fit all their friends, and spend hours swapping stories and telling jokes away from their parents.

"What will we do at this place?" Vickie wondered.

Alexis shrugged the question off. "Eat."

The vampire waited in silence and her expression indicated that she expected a more elaborate answer. "That's it?"

"Well, obviously, we'll talk and hang out and stuff. But yeah, we go there to eat." Alexis had never explained the Friday night hangout to anyone out loud before. She never really had to. When she said it like that, she understood that it sounded boring. "Look, you'll have to trust me on this. It'll be fun. Besides, it's Wisconsin and we're underage. There's not really a whole lot else to do here."

Her father chuckled. "Once you're twenty-one, you'll have a lot more to do. But she's right. As a teen, you're basically stuck with eating."

He was impressed with Vickie. She had spent the remainder of the summer quietly going along with whatever Alexis did. When she told her to do something, she did it and simply assumed that this was what everyone did.

She wanted to be normal and she had nothing to compare it to.

Tonight, however, the vampire showed a little pushback. That told him that she had begun to think for herself, which was not a bad thing. He hoped that she would develop some independence as the school year wore on. *Only the first week of school and she's speaking up. This girl will do fine.* He smiled at her and picked his tablet up again.

The girls arrived in front of Johnny V's. The old, reliable red neon sign with the long, trailing "V" at the end of it gave Alexis a sense of familiarity.

"This is like my second home during the school year," she said to Vickie.

"Don't you want to be home? You spend all week away from home." She didn't quite understand the point of eating someplace different for no reason.

"But our friends are here."

"They're at school, too. We see them all the time. You don't see your dad all week." The old-fashioned dedication to parents burned strongly in Vickie. She believed her status as a young person meant her attention should be on serving her parents, which included her adoptive father.

"Will you question every decision I make?" Alexis smirked. "You have to go with me on this one. This is what everyone else is doing. Trust me."

She didn't have to wait long to learn that the other girl had told the truth. As they walked through the double glass doors of the diner, they were met with a sea of high school kids, most of whom went to Clear Lake.

While she followed without protest, she twisted her face in confusion. *We spent so much time with all these people. Most of my life sciences class is here. Why would I want to see them again?*

Alexis waved at her usual booth in the corner where Jess, Jamie, and Eric waited excitedly for them. Vickie followed her across the diner to the bright red vinyl booth, and they both sat amidst loud greetings.

"So, Vickie, how was your first week at an American school?" Jess asked with a smile.

"It was okay." She nodded. "There's a lot to remember. But I don't think I'm standing out too much."

Jess and Jamie looked at each other with amusement. It was an odd comment to make, but given her international heritage, they simply chalked it up to a simple misunderstanding—as if standing out was a bad thing in her culture.

Of course, they didn't know she was talking about being a vampire. None of them knew that.

Eric would have joined in the "what is she talking about?" silent expression had he been looking anywhere else. But he was fascinated by this girl. He loved her long, dark hair and her crystal-like eyes. Every few moments, he'd catch himself staring and look away, only to find himself staring again minutes later.

"We have to eat here?" Vickie looked at a menu.

Jamie laughed. "Yeah, you can hang out here as long as you eat something. We do dinner here. They make a good burger. And their fries are awesome."

Alexis elbowed her sister. "Yes, but you have to get a shake."

"A shake? What do you mean?"

"It's a drink. It's really called a milkshake, but nobody calls it that. Just ask for a chocolate shake when the server comes by."

The vampire did as she was told. She also ordered a cheeseburger and fries to go with it. Minutes later, two tall cups were placed in front of her.

Neither were recognizable. On the left stood a tall glass filled with a creamy mixture topped with whipped cream and a cherry on top. On the right was an equally tall stainless-steel cup with a spoon sticking out of it. "Why do I have two drinks?"

"It's the same drink," Alexis explained. "The metal can is the leftovers. This is a great place because they make too much to fit into the glass, so they give you the rest. Have a taste."

Vickie jammed the long red straw into the cup and sucked hard until the thick chocolate mixture came up. The sweetness made her sit back and smack her lips together. "Wow, that's a lot of flavor." The group laughed.

"It'll taste even better with a burger," Eric told her, proud of himself for finally mustering up the courage to talk to her.

"But this is ice cream, right?" She looked confused. "Wouldn't you eat this after dinner?"

Alexis raised her index finger. "Actually, if you drink ice cream out of a cup or glass, you can have it with dinner. No, I don't know why. This is another one of those rules that makes no sense when you explain it out loud."

"What do you think of the other students, Vickie?" Jamie asked. "Have you made any other friends? Did you meet anyone?"

Vickie shook her head. "Everyone seems nice, but nobody really talks to me."

"That's because you're new." Alexis took a sip from her own shake. "A lot of the kids like to hang out in their own circles. They have to get to know you a little first. I'm sure everyone will love you."

"Probably not Megan Fitz." Vickie sneered while she pulled her shake closer.

"Ugh." Jess groaned. "Megan Fitz is the worst. Do you have to deal with her?"

"I have her in one of my classes."

"She ran into her in the hallway too." Alexis curled her lip. "Man, I hate her."

"I think Abby and Tiffany are equally as bad." Jess was referring to the two girls with Megan in the hallway.

The server brought five plates of burgers and fries. Vickie stared at the serving in amazement. She had eaten a burger and fries before, but this spread was even more impressive. The burger was massive, and grease dripped off it and soaked into the bun. Not only that, there were so many fries on the plate she couldn't even see it.

"Don't eat the toothpick." Alexis laughed and pointed at the wooden stick with the green paper that protruded from the top of the bun. "That's to hold it together while you get started."

Vickie wrapped her fingers cautiously around the bun and winced at the wet bread from the grease. She sank her teeth into it and her taste buds went crazy. "Mmmm."

"Right?" Her sister smiled. "Now, wash it down with some of that shake. You won't be sorry."

She followed the instructions and gulped some chocolatey goodness. "You do this every week?"

"Just about," Jamie answered and picked up her own burger. "There's nothing better than a burger and a shake at Johnny V's."

The vampire leaned back in her chair for a moment and observed her new friends. While she didn't quite understand the point of getting together on a Friday night yet, she appreciated where she was. *It sure is nice to have a few friends on my side already. I don't know where I would be if I couldn't lean on them to help me get along here. And it definitely helps that I'm not the only one bothered by this Megan girl.*

As she scanned the table, she caught Eric gazing at her again. He smiled awkwardly and returned to shoving fries into his mouth.

From across the table, Alexis laughed. *That dude has the hots for Vickie. I wonder if she knows. She'll be happy to know that, I think.*

For the rest of the evening, the group polished off their meals. Everyone grieved the necessity to go back to school for another year but being able to see each other every day was something to be thankful for.

At the end of the night, Alexis and Vickie walked out the front door with the rest of the group, said farewell to everyone, and wished them a nice weekend.

"Now what?" Vickie asked.

"Now, we go home." Alexis sighed and stared at the stars. "The weekend is usually spent lounging around the house, hanging out with Dad, doing chores, that kind of stuff. And homework. We can't forget to do our homework."

"That doesn't sound like as much fun as this."

"Of course not." She laughed. "Before, you didn't see the point in coming out here. Now, you want to spend all weekend here instead?"

The vampire stuttered something inaudible, unable to answer.

"It's okay. I know, I wish we could hang out all the time too. But it'll be good for my dad for us to be home. This was our first full week away from the house and he had to be alone. He's probably looking forward to having us around to keep him company."

That was a sentiment Vickie could get on board with. She remembered her devotion to her own parents. She wanted to treat her new father with the same degree of respect.

And if spending time with him would make him feel better, that's exactly what she would do. The last thing she wanted was for him to struggle with loneliness, even if he had to deal with his grief a little more directly now that they were home.

CHAPTER SIX

Craig grunted as he shoved the old, heavy wooden desk up against the far wall of his bedroom. The last few inches had been the toughest, but he knew exactly where he wanted it.

For him, it was a very quiet Friday night. The emptiness of the house almost felt like a vacuum. He didn't turn the TV on or any music for background noise, so the only thing he heard were the sounds of his out-of-shape self gasping for air.

Vickie will appreciate the extra space in her room now. The desk—home base for his podcast recording sessions—had originally stood in the spare bedroom. But now that Vickie was living with them, he needed to move it to his room.

That was fine with him. *It's not like I use this room for much anyway. There's no one to disturb in here.*

He walked back to the spare room and wheeled the purple desk chair across the hallway. He spun it around, plopped down in it, and sighed, sounding every bit the old man he felt he was.

Craig grabbed his laptop off the bed, placed it on the desktop, and situated it in the center. He ran his hands along the top of the desk and let its new location sink in.

With nothing left to do, he spun to face the bed. Leaning back in the chair and rocking slightly, he folded his hands and placed them on top of his head. *That bed looks so empty now. The book on the nightstand...the throw pillows... everything is the same. But how can everything look the same and still be so different? Why don't we simply move out of this house?*

Craig knew the answer to that question. There were several reasons, actually.

First, he didn't feel he could handle the stress of selling the house at that point in time. He knew what went into prepping a house for sale, buying a new house, moving...all of that would add additional stress he didn't want to deal with.

Second, despite her efforts to hide it, Craig knew that death was a serious trauma for Alexis to handle. The emotional wallop of moving out of her childhood home would likely be too much to bear. He knew she was already struggling to get used to the new normal life without her mother and he didn't want to add to it.

Finally, there was Vickie. Craig was still unsure of what life looked like with Vickie and he watched out for red flags that would complicate matters.

In short, moving was complicated, and life was complicated enough. As he sat back and stared at the empty bed, Craig decided that was simply a burden he would have to shoulder for the good of his family.

The silence in the house was deafening. Craig got up to

head to the bathroom and blow his nose. The honking that accompanied that particular activity echoed through the house so loudly, he chuckled to himself. *Really, Craig? Is this entertainment now? This is how your wild Friday nights will play out?*

In simpler times, Friday nights were never wild. However, he had looked forward to them. Alexis would be with her friends or possibly hanging out elsewhere in the house. He and Carol would both have their feet up, leaned back in their respective recliners with a movie on the TV.

Maybe they'd finish it. Maybe Carol would fall asleep before it was over. Or she'd fall asleep during the TV show they'd watch after the movie if it was still early enough. Regardless, she always fell asleep first. Craig smiled to himself when he thought about the sound of her light snoring. It used to annoy him. Now, he'd give anything to hear it again.

In the past year, she'd slept a lot more. They watched fewer movies and opted for shorter TV shows where they could watch one or two episodes before she conked out. Chemotherapy was rough on her body, and besides making her feel sick, it wiped out her energy.

Instead of merely listening to her snore, he would roll onto his side and watch her sleep. She had seemed so peaceful. In those moments, he imagined she was free from pain and discomfort, and he loved it. He also knew it was only a matter of time before he wouldn't be able to watch her sleep anymore, so he usually soaked it in as much as he could.

That evening, there was no TV, no movies, and no snoring. Only a man dealing with an empty house.

He walked back into his bedroom and flipped his laptop open to bring up his show notes for an interview he was about to conduct. Jill Riseman, his guest, was very flexible in her scheduling, so he'd booked it for a time when he knew the girls would be out.

She would be the fifth guest on his podcast, *The Truth About...Cancer.* He had spoken to doctors, scientists, other researchers, and various professionals. But he hadn't spoken to a survivor.

Quite honestly, he had mixed feelings about it.

All right, Craig, you know what this woman went through. She's gone through the wringer and it had to be the toughest battle of her life. Whatever you do, don't resent her for it. Just because she beat hers doesn't have anything to do with the fact that Carol lost her fight. This woman is a survivor. Respect her for it.

There were many cancer survivors to choose from. He wasn't merely looking to speak to someone about the experience of fighting cancer. It was something he could talk about and did talk about regularly on the show.

What made Jill Riseman different was that she beat her cancer without chemotherapy or radiation. She made holistic lifestyle changes and claimed that those changes were what cured her disease.

Craig leaned back in his chair again and stared at the picture of the tall blonde with the healthy tan and one-thousand-watt smile. She looked to be at the pinnacle of health—beautiful with an athletic build, clear skin, and a smile that radiated energy.

He glanced at the photo hanging on the wall. In it, he sported a sharp black tuxedo with a white vest and tie, his arms wrapped around the most beautiful woman in the world. Her wavy dark hair fell across her shoulders. She had her own one-thousand-watt smile at the time. It was the one thing about her that never faded.

The woman in that photo had the same energy and vitality that Jill Riseman seemed to have now.

He scrolled through the show notes that contained the bio on Jill he had found.

At twenty-five years old, Jill Riseman was diagnosed with early-stage breast cancer. After reviewing the treatment options available to her, she felt a deep-seated unrest about her future. Four rounds of chemotherapy? Blasts of radiation after that? Hormone-disrupting treatments? It was scary—scary enough that she felt she needed to understand all her options.

After visiting with several holistic doctors, Jill crafted a plan for herself. She changed to a raw, vegan diet consisting mainly of smoothies. She rebuilt her immune system and chose to fight the cancer herself. While her surgery removed the tumor, she rejected all chemotherapy treatments, opting to feed her body rather than poison it.

Six months later, her doctor declared that she was in clinical remission. She believes that her lifestyle changes and choice to take better care of her body contributed to this remission status. Jill beat cancer.

Part of conducting the interview made Craig feel a little uncomfortable. This woman had a blog devoted to her life and beating cancer. He would promote the blog on the podcast in exchange for the interview. As a journalist, he always felt open to exploring all sides of an issue.

But this one hit so close to home with him that it bothered him to hear someone say they beat cancer with "simple lifestyle changes."

As he scanned through the list of changes Jill made to her life, he wondered whether or not Carol would have gone for any of those options.

A raw diet? There wasn't a woman on earth who loved to cook as much as Carol did.

A vegan diet? Nothing came between Carol and a good steak. Nothing. Her favorite season was summer purely because the family fired up the grill every weekend. A tasty, seasoned hunk of beef sliding off the fire could make Carol come running. *I always loved that about her. Marrying a woman who loved steak was the smartest decision I ever made.*

And smoothies? Carol enjoyed them. Craig smiled to himself as he thought of the four-hundred-dollar-plus Vitamix blender that now sat, unused, in the kitchen cabinet. Carol had begged him for it. She wanted to use it to make all kinds of things.

She was a sucker for a kitchen gadget. "But honey," she would say, "it's not only a blender. You can use it to make soups, smoothies, desserts, and so much more." She took on the tone of an infomercial spokesperson. "Soups right in the Vitamix, Craig. No cooking needed."

He loved making her happy, so they sprang for the blender. But as the disease progressed, she lost her energy in the kitchen. Trying out new recipes didn't happen very often, and the Vitamix was put in a cabinet and never came out again.

Imagine if smoothies had really been the ticket to all of this. What if she could have healed her cancer by throwing a bunch of vegetables in that doggone thing? Would she have been grateful, or would she have constantly reminded you of how right she was to get the gadget?

He already knew the answer to that question. Carol loved being right.

Craig shook his head and laughed. *So silly. You can't draw a straight line from one person's cancer treatment to another.*

Still, he prepared himself for the interview. Despite every personal misgiving he had about Jill Riseman's approach, he felt it was his duty to conduct an honest, fair interview with the woman.

He was there to collect the facts and present them to his audience, not pass judgment. *The Truth About...* was an exploratory series, not one that aimed to convince the public one way or the other.

Even that thought made him feel as though he was from days gone by. It seemed every news reporter had some opinion they tried to justify to the audience. He never conducted his investigations that way. Craig felt persuasion was not part of his job description.

As the host of a podcast, he continued that tradition. He would present the facts—or, at least, someone's version of the facts—and let the audience decide for themselves.

He looked again at the wedding photo and smiled at the woman who stared back at him.

If only a few smoothies could have done it. How different his life could have been in that very moment. How much more energy would be in the house.

How much more happiness?

He tapped on the trackpad and opened his video

conferencing software to wait for the cancer survivor to log in and tell him her story.

Craig wasn't sure if it would look silly or look credible, but it would definitely turn a few gears in his head.

What if...

CHAPTER SEVEN

Hundreds of students pushed and shoved their way through the double doors leading to the cafeteria.

Lunch was an area that still left Vickie uncomfortable. School itself was fairly simple—show up to your class on time, find your seat, sit quietly, and answer questions as needed. Repeat for each class until the day was over.

But for her, lunch had a few more moving parts. There was the food line on one end, a small sandwich stand on the other, and several other lines that she wasn't quite sure about.

For someone still trying to figure out the vastly different American food system in the twenty-first century, she had a hard time with the cafeteria.

It didn't help that Alexis wasn't in the same lunch as her. Because Clear Lake High School had over one thousand students, two lunch periods ran back-to-back in the middle of the day.

Alexis was in second lunch. Vickie was in first lunch.

As she walked into the cafeteria, she sighed quietly. *I*

wish Alexis was here. At least I could ask her questions about some of this stuff. I'll make a mental note so I remember to ask her later.

Like the majority of students there, she followed the crowd to the hot lunch line on the far end of the room. There, she walked through a set of double doors where food lines split off to the left and to the right.

She snatched up a blue tray and set it on the railing in front of her, sliding it down as she selected what she wanted to eat from the line. Behind the counter, retirees scooped mashed potatoes into bowls, ladled soup into cups, and picked up chicken fingers with tongs. They passed the food to the students with the ease of many hours of practice.

On that day, Vickie went with a slice of cheese pizza and a large scoop of mashed potatoes smothered in brown gravy. The women serving the meal chuckled to themselves at the odd combination—a reaction that was lost on Vickie.

At the end of the line, she swiped the little meal card and took her receipt before she stepped out into the general chaos of the cafeteria.

Jess and Eric sat near the large windows, two familiar faces who were always welcome sights for her. At least she didn't have to sit alone.

They both smiled as she walked up and set her tray down. Jess chewed a bite of the ham sandwich she'd brought from home. Eric was already partially through his hot lunch, having been one of the first students to reach the cafeteria.

"Don't you get thirsty?" Eric asked Vickie as she took a bite of pizza.

She chewed and swallowed the bite. "Sure."

"Then why don't you drink anything with your lunch? I don't think I could handle eating without having something to drink, even if it's only water."

Vickie gestured to the small vending machine on the opposite end of the cafeteria. "It doesn't take meal credits and I don't really carry money with me."

Jess fought off a snicker. "So? Why would you go to the vending machine?"

"To get something to drink."

She pointed to a shorter line in the middle of the cafeteria. "Just get some milk. They take credits there."

Vickie scanned the sea of students until she noticed one of several lines she'd never really understood. "You can get milk there?"

Eric set his napkin on his tray and stood from his chair. "Come on. Grab your meal card and follow me. I'll show you."

He walked behind Jess, who elbowed him as he passed with a smirk on her face. He rolled his eyes at her and nodded for Vickie to follow him.

"You sounded really lovely this morning," the vampire gushed, barely able to contain her admiration for him.

She was referring to the morning assembly, which was conducted every day. This usually involved a particular life lesson taught to the entire student body by a rotating member of the faculty.

It also served as a way to generate hype for various school activities and sports. If a team won the championship, they ran a trophy presentation ceremony. If they wanted to promote something, they would conduct a free sneak preview.

The music department was gearing up for their fall concert, so Eric was tasked with presenting a tenor solo in front of the entire school. It was a nerve-wracking experience for the boy.

"Oh, thanks. I didn't really…like, I was super-nervous. I don't know if you could tell, but my knees were locked, and all my muscles were clenched with nerves."

I hadn't noticed that at all. I was merely enchanted with your voice. And I sure wish I could actually say those words to you without fear of something bad happening.

They stepped into the milk line, which had shortened considerably since the beginning of lunch.

He pointed to the milk crates at the front of the line. "On that cart are the crates that tell us what is what. You want either the blue one or the brown one."

"What's the difference?"

"The blue one is regular milk, and the brown one is chocolate milk."

"Which one should I choose?"

"Whenever I have the choice, I always go with chocolate milk. Always. Chocolate everything for this guy."

They reached the front of the line, and Vickie bought herself a carton of chocolate milk. "Well, that was easy."

"See? Not so bad."

Instead of returning by the path they had taken earlier, the two continued to walk forward and took the long way around the whole cafeteria. Eric wasn't sure if Vickie could tell what he was doing, but he tried his best to delay their arrival at the table.

"How long have you been a singer?"

"Uh, about a year."

She almost ran into another student who sat at the end of one of the tables. "You've only worked on singing for a year? Not too many humans can say they are that good after only one year." *Shoot, you said humans instead of people. That's okay. Give him a minute. Maybe he didn't notice.*

To her relief, Eric didn't bite on the obvious. "Yeah, my family didn't really pay much attention to music or singing."

"Then why did you join?"

"Ugh. There was this girl. She was in the music department—choir and band, you get the idea. One day, we were singing together. I don't remember what, but soon, she and her friends tried to convince me to join too." He smiled sheepishly. "It was dumb."

"That's not dumb at all. Are you two still together?" *Can I ask that? Too late, I already did. But is that rude?*

Eric shook his head. "I had to break up with her."

"Why?"

He glanced around the room to make sure the other girl wasn't standing there—or one of her friends, just to be safe. "She always tried to one-up me every chance she could. It got really old. If I complained about something, she'd respond with complaints of her own as if it was some kind of game. Well, she always won. Her situations were always worse than mine. I broke up with her because I couldn't handle constantly being reminded about how lousy life can be."

Lousy? Seriously? "That's ridiculous. Look around you. There are planes that fly through the sky. People have phones in their pockets. My goodness, there are even a lot of choices for different kinds of foods. TVs…movies… cars…this whole world is a treasure trove. What would anyone possibly have to complain about?"

Eric looked suspiciously at her. "You don't have these things in Austria?"

Vickie froze. *That's right. I need to remember that they don't know I'm a vampire come back to life. They think I'm only from another side of the world.*

While caught in her momentary confusion, Vickie stared at the young man. He had curly brown hair, and his glasses always slid down his nose. When he smiled, small dimples bordered the corners of his mouth. "It's her loss, then. You are a cute boy who is very nice and friendly. If she couldn't figure out how to be more appreciative of that and see how lucky she was, she doesn't deserve you."

Eric wasn't used to hearing those words. Blood rushed to his cheeks, and his stomach cinched into a knot. "I… uh…thank you." He smiled nervously, completely unsure of how to respond.

She smiled blithely and they stopped in the middle of the cafeteria and simply stared at one another.

"Just kiss her already," a voice called from one of the tables where a group of football players sat.

Eric's eyes widened. He laughed and tried his best to pass it off with something approaching nonchalance. "We should get back to the table. Jess is probably wondering where we are."

Vickie was embarrassed, too. *This is why Alexis told you*

not to say anything like that to him. Now, you've embarrassed him in front of some of the other students. Even if he does like you, coming on strongly will get you in trouble.

As they turned the corner and walked back to the table, Jess looked at them both with her palms up. "Where the heck were you?"

Eric sidled up beside her and sat. "We went to the milk line." He picked his fork up and poked at his mac and cheese.

She raised her eyebrows. "How long does it take to get milk, anyway?"

The other two made eye contact again and shared another nervous smile. Vickie fumbled with the milk carton, not knowing at all how to open it.

"Here, let me help." He reached out to grab the it. Vickie didn't know what he intended to do, so when he took hold, his fingers wrapped around hers for a brief moment.

A twinge of electricity shot down her spine. She released the carton and let him take it. Her eyes narrowed, she watched closely as he peeled open the corner and folded it back to create a small spout she could drink from.

"See? Not so hard." He handed it back to her. This time, their fingers didn't touch, although Vickie wished they did.

She smiled at him. He laughed in response and blushed once more. Then, as if by some unspoken agreement, they both turned their focus to the food in front of them.

"Jess, did you know Eric's girlfriend?" Vickie asked an innocent question, but his eyebrows raised, and he wondered where this conversation was going.

"Oh yeah. Shelly." There was a trace of disgust in her voice. "Crazy redhead."

"Are redheads crazy?"

"Not all of them, but this one sure was. She made all sorts of threats when he broke up with her. Right, Eric? She went way off the deep end. Like, when she found out he had a crush on somebody else, Shelly would go out of her way to try to sabotage any chance he had with the girl. It was stupid. You deserved better than that, man."

"Why do you say that?" Vickie knew the answer to that question, but there was a reason why she asked it.

"Eric's a good dude. He's a nice guy. He doesn't need to be brought down like that. You should be with somebody who makes you happy and is fun to be around. Shelly was neither of those things."

A good dude. That's the kind of language I need to pay attention to. She didn't seem like she was flirting with him, and she didn't make him nervous. Watch your word choice, Vickie.

CHAPTER EIGHT

V ickie struggled to not be overwhelmed by the bright lights that shined at her from all directions.

She, Alexis, and Alexis' father had arrived at the home electronics store. Coming from a world where electricity didn't even exist yet to stare at all the different gadgets and gizmos on display was rough on her senses.

Music piped in from the speakers hanging from the ceiling. TV screens blared along one wall to her right. Ahead of her and toward the back of the store were dozens of different types of computers and tablets organized under bright displays touting their features.

Immediately in front of her was row after row of different kinds of cell phones, and beyond them were aisles of smaller gadgets and even DVDs.

On her left, car technology and appliances towered over the customers walking through.

It felt like a strange, futuristic world.

This is as bad as the airport but different. At the airport, I hadn't seen so many people in my life. But here, it's not people, it's machines.

"I can't believe we forgot to do this," Alexis muttered and shook her head as she walked ahead of her two companions. "Dad, what gives? Why did we wait until weeks into the school year to get Vickie her own computer? It's not like we couldn't afford it."

Her father laughed at her line of thinking. "It had nothing to do with whether or not we could afford it, Alexis. There's an old saying—just because you can doesn't mean you should."

Another one of those old sayings. Be older, Dad. "And what is that supposed to mean?"

He shoved his hands in his pockets. "It means just because we could get Vickie a computer didn't mean it was a good idea. We had to figure that out before we bought one. Otherwise, we'd be wasting money for no reason."

Vickie stopped to watch a video screen that displayed an action camera in use. In it, a man strapped the camera to his chest, took it surfing, and captured a full, 4K picture of the inside of the waves as he rode them. Her jaw hung open while she processed this.

"Did you think we would share my computer or something? Like, all the time?"

Her dad stepped up and put his arm around her shoulder. "Sweetie, when I grew up, computers were a really new thing. I hoped you two could split it. Heck, there was only one computer in my whole house for years."

Alexis laughed. "Dad, don't be so old. Everyone has their own computer now. Besides, Vickie needs to be able to do her own schoolwork on her schedule, and I can do mine on my schedule."

"I know that now, dear. Vickie, come on, let's choose a computer for you."

The vampire dragged her gaze away from the screen and followed them to the back of the store. The laptops were grouped together by brand. The bright, crisp, white display of the Apple computers took up a full third of the computer section of the store.

Because of the clean lines and simple decor, Vickie was immediately drawn to them. There was something pure about them. She picked up a tablet and swiped around on it, then moved to the sleek, metal-colored laptops. The black keys of the keyboard lit up as she pushed buttons and it made her giggle. "These are really nice."

"Yeah, they're also really expensive," Craig said to her. "And for someone who doesn't even know how to use a computer yet, we won't go with those. The one you're touching is over two thousand dollars. Please step away from it very carefully."

Alexis laughed and rolled her eyes while she played with a different tablet. "You don't want to spend too much, eh, Dad?"

"Listen, girls, I'm fine with spending money on a machine you need." He pointed to all the other computers on display. "I don't want to say money is no object. But at the same time, I don't want to pay for something that is grossly overpowered for what you'll do with it. Vickie, you'll write papers, surf the Web, and manage email. It's not like you need a machine that is so fancy it can handle high-end video editing. You won't be doing that. Let's look around some more."

The three split up and wandered the aisles. Vickie didn't know exactly what she was looking for. She merely walked from display to display until she came across the colorful yet clean display of Chromebooks.

The machines looked great, and the display still felt more pure to her. She clicked around and tapped some keys. It felt the same as the Apple computers she had played with a few minutes earlier.

"Now we're talking," Craig said with a laugh as he walked up behind her. "That one you're looking at? That's only four hundred dollars right now, and it's even cheaper for students. That's the kind of computer a dad can get behind."

"Will this do what I need it to do?" She frowned cautiously as she hunched over the keyboard.

"Oh yeah. You're only a student right now. You don't need it to do a lot of fancy things. You simply want it to be reliable, reasonably fast, and something you can do homework on. This fits the bill perfectly, and it's well within the budget I wanted to spend."

Craig flagged a sales rep to unlock the display and get them a computer.

"Dad, I'll show Vickie around a little more."

"Don't buy anything."

The two girls immediately walked over to the wide array of TVs hanging on the wall. They all showed the same sports clips interspersed with highlights of a nature documentary.

The vampire twisted her face in confusion. "What show or movie is this?"

"It's not a show or a movie." Alexis laughed. "This is only a demo reel. It's something they play on TVs in the stores so you can see how the screens look while watching your favorite show or whatever. It's only a demonstration."

Vickie nodded while she watched a Green Bay Packer player burst through the line of scrimmage and cross over into the end zone. A middle-aged man a few aisles over let out a loud "Woo!" at the sight.

"Yeah, so there's something you really need to know if you don't already." Alexis smiled. "You're in Packer Country now. That was an old clip from a game that happened last season, but that guy still cheered. It's not uncommon around here. The season is starting this weekend, and you'll see and hear a lot about the Packers coming up."

"This is American football, right?" The other girl nodded in response. "And you are a big Packer fan, too?"

"Oh yeah. My mom actually grew up in Green Bay, where the Packers are from. She passed that heritage on to me. My dad is, too. Every Sunday, he'll be in his chair watching the game. Most people in this state will be. Every once in a while, someone will throw a party and we'll all get together to watch. It's fun."

Vickie tilted her head. *I hope so. I don't know anything about football.*

"It's easy to watch, too. You'll pick up the rules quickly enough."

As they walked across the store, they stepped through an aisle of DVDs. "What are these?"

"Oh, okay. You know how we watch movies and TV at home using our server? This is, like, the physical version of that." Alexis picked up a copy of *The Fugitive* and explained to Vickie how it worked. "Truthfully, DVDs won't really be around much longer. Neither will Blu-rays. Everybody simply streams their stuff now, like we did in the basement at your castle."

Vickie held the DVD case and studied the box. *So this is what it looks like to hold one of these recordings in your hands. Weird.*

Alexis then led her to her favorite area in the store—the cell phones. The new models were out, and she showed off the beautiful new devices and even snapped a few selfies of the two of them with their tongues out.

Craig walked up behind them holding a bag with a thin box sticking out the top. "What do you think you two are doing?"

"Dad, I already have a phone. Why don't we get Vickie one, too? It doesn't have to be expensive. We should, right?" She winked.

He placed the bag at his feet, straightened, and folded his arms. "Okay, let me ask you something. A couple of months ago, this girl didn't even know what a computer was. She barely knows now, and she'll still have to learn how to use it. You're asking me to get her a second computer and allow her to carry it around with her in her pocket. Does that sound like a great idea?"

"Noooo," his daughter said mockingly.

"These are computers, too?" Vickie lifted one of the phones off the display.

"Basically." Alexis stepped over to swipe the screen and

show her a few apps that were pre-installed on the device. "It's like a small computer, but it also has a great camera built in and it can make calls to other phones. When you want to talk to somebody but they're not here, you know?"

"And you have one, but I shouldn't?"

"For now. It's okay. My dad's right, you should know what you're doing first. Besides, we're together basically all the time when we're not in school. You don't really need one yet."

About half an hour later, the two girls sat on Vickie's bed and pulled the new computer out of its box. Vickie flipped it open and was greeted with a bright white screen and a spinning logo. "I like that. There's something about the color white that always seems so clean to me."

"Go ahead and log into your account. Use the same one you used on my computer. I'll pull your account off mine, and you only have to worry about this machine. This is yours now."

Once she logged in, a web browser automatically popped up with a search bar in the middle. "What should I do first?"

"Type in a question. What's something you have wanted to know since you got here but we haven't talked about yet?" Alexis shrugged. She didn't really know the answer to that. The two of them had covered so much ground in the few months Vickie had been there that Alexis' brain was starting to burst with all the information she had to help out with.

The vampire thought for a moment, then hunted and pecked the keys to type, **how do i know if a boy likes me?** into the search bar.

Looking over her shoulder, Alexis giggled. "Awwww! You could have asked me that one. But let's see what it says."

Hundreds of thousands of search results poured in. "Which one am I supposed to click on?"

"Usually the first few results. But you have to feel it out for yourself. Take some time. This is called Googling. You can Google anything you want. If there's ever anything on your mind, you can pull out your laptop and look it up."

Vickie pecked away at the keyboard until Alexis groaned. "Hang on, let me show you." She placed her fingers on the keys. "Watch and learn. Tell me to type something."

"How about, the rules for American football?" Vickie scratched her chin, her forehead scrunched in thought.

"Perfect." In quick succession, Alexis typed the query and pressed the enter key. Vickie watched her fingers closely to see how they were placed.

"You can type very fast."

"When you know the proper technique, you can too. Did you catch that?"

Vickie watched Alexis type a few more phrases, then closed her eyes for a moment. She opened them, grabbed the computer, and typed flawlessly with her fingers on the proper keys.

"I never get tired of watching you use that rapid learning thing." Alexis shook her head in disbelief and amusement. "Now you have the world at your fingertips."

CHAPTER NINE

The bell rang outside the classroom to tell the student body that the sixth period had begun. For Vickie, that meant world history, one of her favorite classes.

For four hundred years, she had lain in darkness, completely oblivious to what was going on around her. To have a class where she could learn about world events and the culture of society during her sleep was a godsend.

As excited as she was about the class, though, it was initially a little slow for her. The curriculum actually started much earlier, so she learned about events that happened even before she was born.

Still, it held her interest. It was also a favorite because there was no assigned seating. As a result, she rushed to get there early every day so she could locate a seat in the back of the room. *Don't draw attention to yourself. Just blend in.* She had repeated those words so often, they had become a mantra of sorts.

However, her instincts constantly brought more attention to herself without her even realizing it.

Mr. Schroeder, the teacher, was a joyful young man with a red-haired buzzcut and a permanent smile on his face. He taught with energy and enthusiasm and transformed a boring topic into one that somehow included both excitement and relevance for these high school kids.

The subject of that day's lecture was the Peloponnesian War. Vickie recalled studying this before she got to school. Like many subjects, she already knew everything inside and out.

For the average student in this situation, they might grow restless with boredom. But she engaged even deeper with the material, and her enthusiasm almost boiled over at times.

That afternoon, Mr. Schroeder asked for a show of hands. "Who can tell me what brought the Peloponnesian War to an end? Let's see who actually did their homework last night for a change." Her hand snapped into the air. "Vickie? Go ahead and tell us what ended the war."

The words spilled out of her mouth at a rate that seemed almost incomprehensible for the other students. "Sparta received support from the Achaemenid Empire. They supported rebellions in Athens' subject states to undermine the empire and eventually deprived the city of naval supremacy. Once that happened, Athens' fleet in the Battle of Aegospotami was completely destroyed, which ended the war. Athens surrendered the following year, although Sparta refused to destroy the city and enslave its citizens.

"Interestingly enough, did you know that the term 'Peloponnesian War' was never uttered by the historian Thucydides? It is almost universal today because modern historians have strong sympathy toward Athens. The Peloponnesians probably called it the 'Attic War' instead. The event completely changed the Greek world at the time. Sparta was the new dominant force, and Athens went from the top spot to almost the bottom. Poverty ripped through the Peloponnese. Athens was devastated and never again returned to the prosperity it enjoyed before the war, and civil war became a common occurrence in the Greek world."

Mr. Schroeder struggled to keep up with the rambling answer, but it was coherent. Vickie appeared to have all her facts straight. "Um…yeah. That's right." He moved on to another subject and made a mental note to not call on her again too soon.

On the far side of the room, two seats from the front, Jess turned and looked at her friend's cousin. Her eyebrows were raised, and she hoped to catch her eye to tell her to not give such long-winded answers. But Vickie didn't look at her for the remainder of the period.

At the end, the bell rang again, and the students rose to leave for their next classes. Jess met Vickie at the door, and the vampire smiled politely at her. "Holy cow, you are crazy-smart. Where do you learn all this information?"

"I don't know. Books? The Internet? I studied for it. Didn't you?"

Jess laughed. "No, I didn't. But you're practically teaching that class. You're answering Mr. Schroeder's questions before he can even ask them."

"Is that bad?"

"I don't know. I don't think so. You'll probably get made fun of a little more."

Vickie didn't care for that answer. It wasn't that she was afraid someone might say something that wasn't true. It was the extra attention. She wanted to blend in, and this did not meet that goal at all.

She looked at some of the other students. Several made eye contact with her and immediately rolled their eyes. They seemed to make no effort to mask their disdain for her.

After the next class, Jess met up with Alexis.

"Vickie is the smartest person I've ever seen," she almost shouted. "She had so many answers in world history, and half of them were stuff Mr. Schroeder hadn't even taught."

This worried Alexis. "Is she answering too much, or…"

"Probably, if she's worried about that. You should have seen how many people rolled their eyes at her. Oh, man, if looks could kill."

Alexis laughed it off, but her inner concerns remained. *She needs to fit in. What is she doing?*

That night, Craig rolled a few pieces of chicken in a bowl of cornflakes and flour. He had decided to dip back into his old recipe book for one of his favorites. Fried chicken had always been a popular choice in their home.

As the fryer heated and he cut up the chicken, he thought of the dozen or so cookbooks in the hallway closet. Each of them had Carol's name written on it some-where. Despite the temptation to explore them, leafing through those cookbooks would have to wait. He didn't want to be reminded of the family tragedy every time he tried to make dinner.

He collected recipes—like fried chicken—and did his best to make his own favorite meals while he allowed himself the time he needed to adjust. Maybe down the line, he'd be ready to go through those recipes and make a few of them. Right now, he wasn't ready.

At the kitchen table, Vickie and Alexis set up plates, laid out potholders, and distributed silverware to each place setting.

"I hear you're doing well in your classes." Alexis looked up and tried to keep her expression casual.

"Really?" Vickie leaned forward, excited. "How good?"

"Too good."

"What does that mean? How can something be too good?"

The other girl walked to the fridge to grab the gallon of milk in the door. "If you answer questions the teacher hasn't even asked yet, you're probably too good."

The oil in the fryer popped and crackled a few times when Craig raised the lid to add the breaded chicken. The oil bubbled furiously at first, then settled into a gentle rumble. The smell of fried chicken filled the air almost instantly.

Alexis continued her explanation. "You don't want to sound too smart to people. If you want to fit in, you can't raise your hand for every question in class."

Vickie looked out the bay window in the kitchen. "I can't get good grades? I can't be smart?"

"I didn't say that. I said, 'too smart.' You need to fit in, and you can do that and get good grades."

"Hang on a second," her father interjected. "What is Vickie doing that is so terrible? Is she really looking that bad in class?"

Alexis turned to her father and told him the story about the Peloponnesian War question that Jess had related. The vampire watched, dumbfounded, as Craig reacted very similarly to everyone else—with a groan and a sneer.

"Why is it so bad if I know the answer to something?"

"It's not that, Vickie." Craig lifted the basket and shook it to check on the chicken in the fryer. "You're simply standing out more than you want to. See, as a vampire, you have to constantly remind yourself that your brain works far more quickly and efficiently than a regular human's brain does. If you retain all the information you read or learn, you're already way ahead of other kids. They—and the teachers—will notice and want to know more about you. Look, I get it. I was a super-nerd, myself. Dare I say it, a mathlete."

"What's wrong with that? What's a nerd or a mathlete?"

Alexis giggled. "It's Dad's finest moment in life so far. It means you answer every question right away, you look forward to homework…you're basically jazzed about learning."

"I still don't think I understand why this is such a big deal. Doesn't everyone want to strive to do this well?"

"Absolutely." Craig lifted the basket again, this time satisfied with how dark the chicken was. He flipped the pieces onto a paper-towel-lined plate. "And you will make friends, but we'll have to figure out how to balance that with not drawing excessive attention."

"Normally, that's not a problem for mathletes," said Alexis.

Vickie looked at the other girl. "No offense to… anybody, but yeah, I do want more friends here. It gets lonely. And I do have Jess, Jamie, and Eric already."

Alexis shook her head. "But those are my friends, although you can hang out with them all you like. I don't care. But you also do need to have your own life. We can't be joined at the hip for the rest of our lives. We can help you, but you have to make new friends of your own who like what you like."

"Where do I find these people?" She put her hands on her hips and looked faintly challenging.

"In the computer lab, most days, or the robotics teams." Alexis looked at her father who arched an eyebrow at her. "What? You know I'm right."

"It's all about the tone, dear daughter." Craig dropped a handful of French fries into the basket of the fryer and loaded it into a sizzling bowl of oil. "I want to keep you safe, which for now, means not standing out. That's why we're asking you to be a solid B student. Good but not so great that teachers mention you in the lounge."

"What am I supposed to do? I have all this knowledge and I know the answers. Are you telling me that I have to suppress my ability? To lie?"

"We're not asking you to throw your smarts away." Alexis pulled out a kitchen chair and sat. "We only want you to do what I call pacing yourself. You don't want to go too fast, so you pace yourself. You keep your mouth shut occasionally, and you pick and choose the times when you let your brain go crazy and answer everything."

"When would that be?"

"For now, here at home when you're safe with us. We're all new at this, including you despite your age. If this were to get out…" Craig let the idea hang between them for a moment.

"I get it," said Vicki. "I need to become the observer more. Learn American teenage culture, maybe, instead of diving right in."

"Now that's using that ginormous brain of yours," Alexis said approvingly.

It was another day and another warning for Vickie. *In honor of you, Father. I can do this.* She remembered that last moment together. *You told me goodbye and didn't show your fear.* Even though all of Salzburg wanted him dead.

If he can stay calm and in control of his abilities, then I can too.

That reminder gave her a renewed commitment to not out herself as a vampire and put her new family in danger.

She needed to tap into that inspiration directly so she wouldn't be tempted to use her powers in front of people. Her father had already given her the blueprint to follow. She now needed to listen to it and follow it.

CHAPTER TEN

That evening, though, when she sat alone in her room, she sighed quietly.

I really wish I could be open with my powers. Sometimes, I feel like I betray my own lineage by being here and trying to live like a human. Every instinct I have is inappropriate now. What good is it being a vampire when you're surrounded by people who not only aren't what you are but would also throw you in prison or murder you if they found out you were one?

Yet, if she thought about it, not much had changed in four hundred years. She hadn't been an overt vampire before her sleep. She'd still had to hide herself and her powers. The era might be different, but the truth remained the same as it had been for centuries. If you were a vampire, you could not be open about it or you would face dire consequences.

She walked down the hall to the bathroom to brush her teeth. Staring in the mirror, she bared her teeth and scrubbed them with the brush to keep them pearly white.

When she came to her fang teeth, she took extra special care to get them clean.

Once she'd rinsed and spat, she dabbed her mouth dry and bared her teeth again. She ran her tongue along the top row and felt the slight sharpness of her fangs, which were retracted.

Craig walked past with a smile on his face and poked his head in. "Hey, hey. Careful with those things. I don't want to see any bite marks on your pillows tomorrow morning." With a chuckle, he walked away.

Vickie smiled at first, but once he'd left, the smile slowly faded. An overwhelming sense of loneliness crept in. *He was only joking. You know that. He meant no harm by it. But it's another reminder of how everyone expects me to hide. There is no option for me to simply be a vampire. I'm the last one. No one knows what it's like to be a true vampire, and there isn't anyone I can share this with.*

She flipped the bathroom light off, walked to her bedroom, and shut the door behind her. Her laptop in hand, she crawled into bed. The light from the screen provided the only illumination in the entire room.

With slight hesitation, Vickie opened the web browser and clicked in the search box to type **do vampires exist?** before she pressed the enter key.

Page after page came up. At first, she saw pages dedicated to the lives of vampires, the history of vampires, and even "modern" vampires.

That last one disgusted her. *There are people in this world who choose to drink blood? And they think that makes them vampires? I'm both grossed out and offended. How dare they think the only thing vampires do is drink blood? And even so, merely drinking it doesn't mean you're a part of the struggles and history of my people. Ugh.*

One article, however, introduced a term that she had never been familiar with—Sanguinarians.

She returned to the search box and typed in, **what are Sanguinarians?**

One of the first pages that popped up was titled, **Sanguinarians vs. Vampires.** *This should shine a light on things.*

The page first detailed what exactly a vampire was. In this, there were no surprises—other than Vickie being surprised at how accurate it was. *Whoever wrote this did the right research. I guess there are people in today's world who understand what real vampires are. Or were, I guess.*

According to the author of the article, vampires were supernatural beings who possessed heightened abilities and awareness and added that some written historical accounts claimed they had super-speed.

This article also contained a snippet that won Vickie over immediately.

While many people have claimed that vampires suck blood, this is a detail lost in history for some reason. True vampires did not subsist on blood, nor did they drink it. They had fangs and possessed supernatural powers, but that is where the similarities between the pop-culture vampire and the real-world vampire end.

. . .

Vickie smiled with real approval. *Well put, but why do people think that, then, anyway?*

She continued reading.

True vampires disappeared from historical records several hundred years ago, right around the time of the Sang Crusade (see below). To this day, there remains no evidence that any true vampires have existed for at least 300-400 years. Some historians believe they were victims of the Sang Crusade, although they were not direct targets.

This information made sense to Vickie but was also somewhat puzzling. *Okay, so at this point, I'm the last vampire on Earth. I'd worked that out for myself. I haven't sensed any others. But what is this Sang Crusade, really? Is that what the Circle was all about?*

She didn't have to wait for an answer.

The Sang Crusade, a religious and military effort conducted by a religious group known as the Slayer Circle during the Thirty Years' War, targeted Sanguinarians.

They are closely related to what we consider to be vampires today. Called Sangs for short, these creatures bore a striking resemblance to both humans and vampires. The key difference between the races, however, is that Sangs were known to feast on human blood and flesh.

· · ·

"Biters," Vickie whispered to herself. "Sangs were biters."

During the Crusade, men from the Circle marched through cities and towns throughout Europe and mercilessly slaughtered all Sangs and vampires they came across. The Circle believed they had a higher calling to destroy the Sang race and protect humans from these creatures that feasted on them.

However, also during that time, it was believed there was no difference between the Sangs and vampires. The Circle, along with most other groups—particularly religious groups—treated both races as one and the same. They were all grouped together in discussions about the supernatural beings.

Over time, this resulted in the general term vampire being used to describe any supernatural being that sucked blood. Pop culture latched onto this description and the modern image of a vampire was hatched from this generalization.

While this explanation made all the sense in the world—and some of it was already known to her—Vickie couldn't help but feel insulted. People who didn't care to differentiate lumped her family in with the biters, giving the vampire race a bad name.

In her day, biters and vampires didn't associate with each other. While they possessed similar characteristics, their outlooks couldn't have been more different.

Biters were notoriously violent and confrontational. They believed war needed to be waged between themselves and humans, and they wanted to rule over the humans and use them as sustenance. Humans, of course, weren't interested in that idea.

Vampires, on the other hand, wanted to live peacefully. But because of the similarities between biters and vampires, they were soon all lumped together.

This was why her father was so particular about them hiding their powers when out in public...exactly like she had to be in the present day.

Vickie leaned back from her computer and rested her head on her pillow to stare at the glow from the device shining on the ceiling. *People didn't want to learn any more about us. They made up their minds and used that prejudice to wipe us out, even though we didn't do anything. I don't know whether to be angrier at the Sanguinarians or at the humans who killed us all.*

There was one interesting piece missing in that article. While the author made sure to mention that the vampire race was wiped out, nothing was specified about the Sang race. *Are there any more biters out there? Like, real ones, not people who pretend to be biters?*

After Googling a little more, she came across an article that made an interesting point.

While the true vampire race was considered wiped out by the 17th or 18th centuries, there are no definitive accounts that the Sangs were also exterminated. Some believe Sanguinarians did survive the Crusade and

continue to walk among us to this very day, hidden in plain view.

This was an interesting thought to Vickie. Were there still biters around? What would happen if she came across one? Would there be hostility? And how had they remained hidden so effectively all this time?

She spent another hour searching the Web in a concerted effort to find any definitive proof that Sangs were gone. But while she did find more and more articles claiming the vampires were extinct, nothing truly proved that Sangs were confirmed to be extinct.

Vickie closed her laptop, plugged her charger in, and slid it under her bed for the evening. It was after 11:00 pm, and she had to be up early in the morning for school.

The thoughts continued to nag at her and prevented her from falling asleep.

She didn't know how to feel about the idea that biters were still out there. Of course, she hadn't known any directly and had only heard stories about them from her father. Would biters be receptive to her? Could she bond with them with the understanding that the world considered them all vampires?

Although she was the only remaining true vampire, could she at least feel a camaraderie with biters, knowing that they, too, lived in hiding?

Or, if they knew she was the lone survivor of her race, would they simply try to kill her so they could exert their own perceived dominance over the race?

Thoughts and ideas swirled through her head as she

tossed and turned in her bed, irritated by her active mind and the covers that seemed to rumple and twine around her legs. Ultimately, she decided it was a lost cause.

Even if they do exist, what are the chances that any biters are hanging out here in America? It's probably only some Internet rumor. Alexis says not everything you read on the Internet is true. Somebody could have made this up to get a laugh. The odds of you running into one are slim to none.

Worse, all this thinking about biters really did nothing to comfort or soothe Vickie or solve her real problem. In this new world, where she lived peacefully and quietly among humans, she had to fight her instincts at every turn. If she wanted to fit in and simply survive, she couldn't do the things that came naturally to her.

Whether or not biters existed anymore had no significance for the true problem.

She merely wanted to be herself, and she didn't see any way that could be possible in her new life.

Although that thought filled her with an intense sadness that felt like a weight sitting across her chest, accepting it quieted the questions in her mind long enough to fall asleep for the few hours of rest that remained.

That night, however, she dreamed of a normal day in her home castle, surrounded by her siblings and her parents. Vickie was a kid again and raced through the house in play with her brother and sister.

She ate dinner with her family and enjoyed her parents' warm smiles from across the table.

As brief as the rest had been, it provided a small break from the stress and concern of the present-day world.

She'd needed it, even if it was nothing more than a vision of days long gone.

83

The girls stepped out of the car in the parking lot of the school to see a wild commotion in progress near the back entrance. Vickie's stomach tightened instinctively.

"What on earth is going on this early?" Alexis ran in the direction of the crowd. "Come on."

The two reached the group of kids that yelled and pushed each other for a better view. In the middle of the circle, two junior boys threw punches at each other.

"What's the deal?" Alexis asked one of the spectators.

"Paul caught his girlfriend cheating with Zack and told him he was gonna beat him up this morning."

Paul was a two-hundred-pound football player, and Zack was a smaller boy on the soccer team. They traded punches unrelentingly. While Zack stood his ground, Paul was simply too powerful for him.

The smaller boy will be seriously hurt. I need to stop this before that happens. Vickie inched forward but Alexis grabbed her arm and pulled her back.

"No." She stuck her index finger in the vampire's face. "You can't."

"They won't hurt me."

"Exactly." Alexis' eyes were wide and serious. Even though Paul was sure to do serious damage to Zack, Vickie could not intervene.

The vampire gritted her teeth while they watched Paul shatter Zack's nose and hurl the boy to the concrete in a bloody heap. As he delivered the knockout blow, one of the teachers sprinted out of the rear entrance.

The onlookers, including the two girls, scattered. Once they were a safe distance away, they resumed a normal walking pace.

"You should have let me do something." Vickie shook her head angrily. "I could have defused the situation."

Alexis stepped in front of her, stopped walking, and forced her to halt in her tracks. "You wouldn't have defused anything. What you would have done was demonstrate your super-strength in front of a dozen of your classmates. You would have made things worse."

Vickie continued to walk and bubbled with frustration. *What good are these powers if I'm never allowed to use them? Even to help people.*

The girls separated as they walked into the school building. They would meet up in the hallways in a few minutes, but first, they each needed to visit their lockers.

It was 6:30 am. In the morning, they always caught a ride with Jess and her older sister. The halls were empty, as few people came to school earlier than they had to.

Jess's sister, Ashley, always came this early. The parking lot had a limited number of spaces. Once those spaces were full, students had to park on the Honey Creek Parkway behind the school building.

The parkway was separated from the school's view by a bank of trees. It was where students liked to sneak off to if they wanted to indulge in misbehavior. Some would smoke and boys brought girls back there—only two of a long list of rule breaking. If your car was parked there, it might provide cover for someone who had no desire to be seen.

That was the best-case scenario. Down the road from the high school was the public school for kids who had been kicked out of every other high school in town. Often, some of those students would leave campus to break into the cars on the parkway, where nobody could see them until it was too late.

Ashley didn't want to deal with either of these problems, so she parked close to one of the school entrances. That meant arriving nice and early, which she didn't mind.

The *bang* when Vickie's locker door slammed shut echoed down the nearly silent corridor. She slipped her arms through the straps on her backpack and walked toward the small hallway off the main area of the downstairs lobby.

This was home to the less-popular classrooms, like the Home Economics and Family Living rooms. Nobody hung out in them during the morning, so other than staying out of the way of lockers, kids could hang out in that hall and not be disturbed.

Eric greeted her as she approached.

"What are you doing here so early?" Vickie asked. "Doesn't your mom drop you off?"

"Yeah, she does." He sighed, and his words slurred

somewhat from fatigue. "I have a doctor's appointment after school today, so I had to get my miles in this morning since I won't be at practice later."

"What practice?"

"Cross country. I'm a runner."

"Where do you run?"

"All over." He laughed. "Cross country is distance running. So at practice, we go out for runs. Coach tells us to get in six miles, and we go six miles."

"How many miles did you run this morning?"

"Five. It was a standard day. I knew it would be, that's why I asked my mom to schedule the appointment for today. If it had been seven or eight miles, or if we had a hard workout planned, I would have stayed. But I can knock out five miles by myself, no problem."

The gears turned slowly in Vickie's head. "How do you join the cross country team?"

He shrugged. "Talk to Mr. Lueck. He's the coach. I think this late in the game, you'd have to try out. We've been running together since the summer." He tried to contain his eagerness to have her on the team. Even if they wouldn't run side by side, he'd have a lot more opportunities to hang out with her if she were on the team.

For her part, Vickie was eager too. She remembered Eric's story of joining the choir to be near a girl. *Maybe I could join cross country to be near him. Would that be too obvious? Can I even be a cross country runner?*

"What are the rules?" she asked. "Like, how do you know what to do during a cross country game?"

He snickered and tried not to sound like he was making fun of her for not knowing. "It's not like that. First of all, it's called a meet, not a game. And there aren't really many rules. You simply run. There's a path you have to follow—that's called a course. As long as you stay on the course, you're following the rules, I guess."

She smiled. *I like that. Not a lot of rules to remember and I already know how to run. This could be the perfect thing for me.* "But where's the challenge, then? It sounds boring."

"Oh, brother. Well, you must be in pretty good shape. Distance running is tough. It requires a lot of endurance. Maybe there aren't a lot of rules to follow, but you have to be in really good shape to cover those distances without burning out."

"Are you in good shape?"

He blushed. "I'm okay. I'm an average runner, but I have to work hard to stay average. There are other guys on the team who are way better than me. Chris and Micah, the team captains, are naturals. They're in great shape. I do my best."

Vickie scanned her memory to see if she knew anything else about cross country. She remembered seeing a handful of students running outside on the day she came into the school for her placement testing. Seven or eight boys ran furiously in circles while a man with long black hair held something in his hand and shouted to them as they ran. "Do you run around that circle outside? I think I've seen some kids doing that."

Eric laughed. "That circle is the track. It's where we do really tough speed workouts. Those are the workouts where Coach Lueck runs us so hard, we puke." She grimaced in disgust and Eric immediately regretted saying that. Blood rushed to his face. "Yeah, it's not great. I don't like puking. But you know, it's what happens when you run really hard."

You won't impress her with how hard you run, dude. "I'm not the only one, either. A lot of the guys puke during hard workouts. It's normal." *Her expression hasn't changed. Talk about something else.* "Yeah, one time last winter, he ran us so hard, we all threw up." *Man, stop talking about puking. What are you doing?*

"I don't want to throw up." Vickie stared ahead and avoided eye contact with him. "That doesn't sound like fun."

"The girls don't. He only runs the guys like that. Anyway, we don't usually run on the track. Like I said, those are only for hard workouts. Usually, we run out on the trails. Sometimes, we run along the creek under the parkway. At other times, we run through neighborhoods. The seniors usually lead the runs."

They reached the place in front of the Home Ec office door where they usually hung out before school. No one entered or exited that office in the mornings, so it provided a quiet place between two banks of lockers where they could relax, talk, and avoid most of the hustle and bustle of the morning arrivals.

Jess was already seated there, reviewing some of her homework for the day. She was a morning person. Alexis hadn't arrived yet.

"Hey, Eric." Jess greeted him with a smile. "Ready for the big chem exam today?"

"I hope so." He dropped his overstuffed backpack onto the floor beside her and lay down to rest his head on the backpack like a pillow. "I was up half the night studying. I need sleep." Within two minutes, he was out cold.

"Does he sleep here every day?" Vickie asked.

The other girl smiled and shook her head. "Basically. He doesn't sleep a lot at home. Sometimes, I think he's more awake than he lets on. Like he pretends to sleep or something. But whatever he wants to do. Are you doing okay today?"

"I guess so." She leaned against the wall beside the lockers and slid down until she sat on the floor and hugged her knees. "I'm simply trying to figure out where I fit in."

Jess waved her hand airily. "Don't worry too much about that. You have some friends here already, so that makes life a little easier. Keep being you and you'll do fine. Everyone has a place to fit in here. It'll happen naturally."

Vickie didn't really like that answer. She knew Jess tried to be encouraging. But with all the uncertainty surrounding her life, she wanted to actually find some answers.

Alexis walked up and sat next to her. "Whatcha talking about?"

"Fitting in." Vickie rested her head back on the side of the lockers. "I want to make friends but I honestly don't really know how yet."

"What do you mean? You have friends right here. What am I?" Alexis placed her hand on her chest. "I have your back around here. How many friends do you need?"

Vickie rolled her eyes. "That's not what I mean. I know you're my friend. I just… I feel like I tag along with your friends and your group. Your life. I need to do something that's *mine*."

Jess looked up from her homework. "You want an identity."

"Exactly. I like you guys and I like hanging out with you, but I don't know who I am yet. Does that make sense?"

Alexis remained silent. She honestly had mixed feelings despite the fact that she had been the one who told Vickie to find new friends. *I didn't know it would be so easy to leave us behind.*

"No, I get it," Jess said and nodded. "We've all hung out with each other for a while now, and we found ourselves organically. You kinda hang out with us by default because you don't know anyone. That's okay. And you can hang out with us as long as you like. But if you want to make other friends, we understand. Right, Alexis?"

Her sister shot her a frustrated look.

"Thanks." Vickie smiled and looked at the floor. "I'll keep hanging out with you, but I also want to be able to develop my own life. I haven't done that in centuries."

Jess laughed, thinking the centuries comment was a joke. "It's probably felt like it, right?" She beamed a bright smile.

The other two girls nodded and avoided eye contact, realizing that Vickie slipped up. They both flashed awkward smiles to pass it off as a joke, too.

"What if I joined a sport?" the vampire asked.

Alexis looked unsure about it. *If you can't control your powers, you will reveal yourself very quickly. But I can't say that to you out loud.* "Getting involved in something is the quickest way to make friends. We all got to be friends from being in choir together. I don't know if sports is your thing or not, but I guess that's something we can talk about."

The first bell signaled to the students that it was time to head to their first period classes. Eric's body twitched as he shook awake.

"Let's go, sleepyhead," Jess joked and kicked him playfully with her toe.

He dragged himself to his feet and blinked his bloodshot eyes a few times. "Fine, let's go." He smiled at the sisters, then turned and walked with Jess to their first classes of the day.

"It's not us, is it?" Alexis asked her.

"What?"

"Do you not like my friends?"

"Oh, it has nothing to do with that." Vickie placed her hands on Alexis' shoulders. "It's all about me. I don't really know how to explain it. I need…something. I don't know what that is yet."

The two of them walked to the stairs and went their separate ways to start their morning.

CHAPTER TWELVE

The morning had been uneventful. Vickie cruised through her classes as usual and sat with Jess and Eric for lunch.

Watching the two friends interact made her uncertain about him. There was almost a flirtatious energy to their relationship. They were very comfortable around each other, and secretly, she wondered if they were dating.

They would laugh at each other, elbow one another playfully, and hugged every day. The vampire was not familiar with how social interaction played out, and the situation confused her.

As if that wasn't bad enough, she seemed doomed to face even more confusion.

She took a bite of her spaghetti and a thin mustache of sauce slopped onto her upper lip. Before she could grab a napkin to wipe it off, a tall, broad-shouldered boy with buzzed blonde hair walked up to the table.

He wore a blue jacket with C's and L's stitched onto the arms. Safety pins lined the left breast, and another large C was stitched onto the opposite. He wore tight jeans and kept his hands shoved into his pockets.

That's a good-looking guy. What's he doing here? Do I know him somehow? No, I would remember him. Is there anything on my face? Is that why he's here?

"Hey." He smiled awkwardly at Vickie.

"Hey."

"I'm Steve."

"I'm Vickie."

"Yeah, I know. I've watched you since you got here. New girl, right? Came from Germany?"

She smiled sheepishly. "Austria, actually."

"Austria, right. Hey, do you want to get together for… like, some food on Friday night? Maybe go to Johnny V's and grab a burger?"

Vickie looked at Eric. He stared at Steve and wore a mixture of confusion and annoyance on his face. He didn't seem to be a fan.

Jess, on the other hand, was both impressed and excited. Her jaw slightly open, she made eye contact with Vickie and nodded slightly to encourage her to accept.

"Sure. Sounds like fun."

"Awesome. Be there at seven. It's a date." He turned and walked away. She watched him for a moment, and girls at all the tables between them looked constantly from Steve to Vickie in disbelief that this had actually happened.

"Girl," Jess nearly shouted in excitement. "You got yourself a first date."

"What does that mean?"

"It means you'll spend a little more time getting ready on Friday night. That big hunk of meat is Steve Miick. He's the running back for the football team. He's a babe, and he's popular. He doesn't walk around asking out anybody. This is huge. Do you know how many girls would kill to be you right now?"

Vickie was still confused by the whole thing. As she scanned the cafeteria, she noticed several girls staring at her in disbelief, and more than a few glared daggers at her. *I guess I have a date.*

Eric spent the rest of the lunch eating quietly and didn't say much of anything. His gaze remained fixed on the table.

That Friday evening, Alexis stood behind Vickie in the bathroom and ran a straightener through her hair. "I know you already have straight hair, but this will make sure it's super-straight. Nice and clean, that's what you want."

"I'm nervous." The vampire giggled. "I don't know what to expect here. We only arranged marriages back in my day. This dating thing didn't really exist."

"Okay. Well, as long as you don't end up marrying the guy tonight, you'll probably be in good shape." Alexis ran another section of her hair through the straightener carefully as steam rose from her hair. "Go and have a nice time. Don't overthink it."

"Have you ever been on a date before?"

Alexis paused. It was a point of frustration with her. "No, I haven't. But someday, I will. That's not something I spend much time worrying about, anyway. I know if I simply be myself, the right guy will come along. I'm excited for you." She was hardly convincing in her tone, but Vickie didn't pick up on it.

In the car on the way to Johnny V's, Craig drove rather quietly. Dating was not a topic he was prepared to discuss, especially with the four-hundred-year-old vampire and especially so soon into this experiment. Instead of trying to fumble his way through the discussion, he tried to ignore it as much as possible.

As the girls exited the car, he wished them both fun. "Alexis." His daughter leaned over and stuck her head back into the car. "Keep an eye on her, okay?" He didn't elaborate on what he meant but his eyes told her everything she needed to know.

She nodded. "I'll make sure of it, Dad." *That's one scared man. Poor guy.*

He drove off, and the two of them walked into the restaurant. Alexis waved at Jess and Jamie in the back of the room. "There are the girls. They're at our usual table. I don't know where you're supposed to go but hang out by the door and he'll show up or something. I'll be right over there if you need anything, okay?"

The butterflies danced in Vickie's stomach. "Okay. I'll let you know."

"Hey." She faced Vickie and looked her directly in the eye. "Relax. Have fun. And be yourself—without the vampire stuff." She winked and walked to the booth where her friends waited.

For about ten minutes, Vickie hovered at the front of the restaurant and waited for Steve to arrive. Every time the door opened, she looked eagerly to see who walked through, but it was never him.

An old woman who worked at Johnny V's approached her. "Can I help you with something, sweetheart? You've stood here for quite a while."

"Oh, I'm waiting for someone." She pointed to the door. "I'm sure he'll be here any minute."

The old woman nodded. "I'll tell you what, why don't we sit you down at this table over here? You can watch the door, and as soon as he comes, he'll see you waiting for him. That way, you don't have to pace around and wear yourself out so early in the night, dear."

"Thanks." Vickie followed her to a small, two-person table and she sat quickly. She turned down the woman's offer to get her something to drink. Instead, she sat and tapped her foot while she watched and waited for Steve.

A few more minutes turned into half an hour. Time marched on. Soon, Vickie looked up at the clock on the wall. It was 8:20 pm.

She didn't know how to react, so she continued to watch the door. Steve never showed.

Alexis shuffled over to the table and sat. "I don't think he's coming."

"No, I don't think so either." Vickie's face fell. "I think I want to go home."

"I've already called my dad. Let's get out of here."

The two girls stood. With baseless hope, Vickie looked at the sea of high school students at various tables all over the restaurant. *Maybe he's sitting at another table, waiting for me to arrive.*

He wasn't there but she made eye contact with Megan Fitz, who sat with a group of other girls at a large booth in the corner of the restaurant. All the girls laughed and joked and glanced constantly at Vickie.

Megan gave her a cocky smile. Vickie scowled at her, turned, and headed out of the restaurant.

***

After a quiet weekend, they arrived at school on Monday. Throughout the day, Vickie felt as though she was on display. Everywhere she walked, it seemed somebody whispered about her.

Word had spread across the school that she had been stood up by Steve Miick. She didn't see him anywhere all morning.

Until lunch.

She sat at the table and barely said a word as she scarfed her chicken sandwich. Across the table, Eric watched her with concern and wished she hadn't been so hurt. *If Steve Miick wasn't a big football player, I would go find him and punch him square in the nose. What a jerk.*

"Oh, no..." Jess trailed off as she looked off into the distance, then to Vickie.

"What?" Vickie looked up and in the direction Jess indicated. To her surprise, Steve walked with Megan, hand in hand. The other girl made eye contact with her, stuck her tongue out, and raised her hand to show their fingers interlocked. Steve saw her and laughed, and the two of them continued, their amusement at her expense blatant.

Anger built up Vickie's body. Her senses heightened, and she could hear every snide comment the girls made across the cafeteria.

"What was she thinking? Like she really had a shot with him?"

"Everyone knows Steve and Megan are dating. Did she think she would break them up?"

"I can't believe she fell for that."

"How embarrassing."

"Welcome to America."

Vickie stood from the table and walked away to throw the rest of her food in the garbage. She power-walked out of the cafeteria, still carrying her empty tray.

At the threshold, she paused and scanned the hallway to find a quiet corner in which she could be alone. She walked past a few groups of friends who milled about until she turned the corner in the Band Hall and found no one there.

The vampire marched to the middle of the hallway and took a deep, cleansing breath. She lifted the tray and snapped it in half, and a few pieces of blue plastic fell to the floor.

A trash can stood nearby, and she walked over to it and held each half of the tray above it in separate hands. She squeezed as hard as she could to shatter the remains and allowed them to fall into the garbage.

The bell rang, and she took another deep breath to calm herself. Her fangs retracted, and she resumed the rest of her day.

***

That night, the two girls sat on the back porch, enjoying the sunset on one of the few remaining beautiful nights in Wisconsin before winter set in.

"I'm sorry about Steve." Alexis put her hand on her sister's shoulder. "I'm sure it hurt."

Vickie shrugged. "I'm not heartbroken. I'm more mad than anything else. I want revenge on him. And on Megan, who had to be behind all of it."

"Oh, I'm positive she was. I didn't know they were dating either, though. That part doesn't surprise me. He's kind of a jerk."

"Why didn't you tell me he was a jerk?"

"He was your first date. I didn't want to ruin it for you. Some things, you have to learn on your own. And you were excited. I wanted to encourage that."

She stared at the setting sun and frowned.

"Don't let it get to you," Alexis insisted. "She wanted to be mean. That's all it is. You're better than that."

CHAPTER THIRTEEN

The next day was unsettling for Vickie. After dealing with her first taste of high school drama, it seemed as though everyone now watched her closely.

Word had spread like wildfire overnight through social media that Vickie had been duped into a fake date with Steve Miick.

The second she walked through the front doors, people stared at her and talked under their breath about how embarrassing the whole ordeal must have been for her.

Alexis had even warned her during breakfast that morning.

"I've been online this morning. Everybody is talking about it, but don't let it get to you. People are idiots. They're only looking for something to talk about because they don't have anything going on."

Vickie shook her head all morning, each time she encountered yet another whispering huddle. "I don't know why someone would do that to someone else."

As she walked through the halls, her gaze darted from

person to person. How quickly she had gone from an anonymous newcomer to the victim of a very public prank. She had a recognizable face for all the wrong reasons.

What bothered her the most, however, was when a pack of girls stood at one end of the hallway and stared at a video on a phone and laughed. When they saw her approach, they tucked it away quickly and bolted the scene.

Between two of her classes, Alexis tracked her down to speak in hushed tones.

"Vickie, Megan recorded the whole thing and shared it online. It's all over the place. I'm sorry. Whatever you do, don't watch it. The last thing we need is for you to go crazy and kill the girl for doing something this stupid. We'll figure it out, okay?"

The vampire felt like she was in some sort of trance. She had grown numb to the embarrassment and didn't even respond when Alexis warned her of the video. Instead, she simply nodded and walked away.

Her sister stood in the middle of the hallway with her hands on her hips. *Please don't lose it over this. It's garbage. Let it be. You can overcome this. Don't let high school eat you alive already.*

During her class with Megan, they occasionally made eye contact. The girl would smile cockily, while Vickie frowned in response. Her fangs would poke out ever so slightly, and she did her best to shake off her frustration.

Don't let something this stupid be why you out yourself. Keep things in check. Be better than this.

After the last bell rang and she'd packed her things up, she met Alexis outside on the steel benches in front of the school building. A steady stream of cars drove up to the curb to pick students up and take them home.

The sun was shining, and Alexis leaned back with her face tilted to the sky and her legs crossed. "Soak in that sun, Vickie. Enjoy the warmth. The dark days of winter will be here, and you'll think they will never end."

Vickie rested her elbows on her knees, hunched over, and stared at the ants crawling around her shoes. "Is winter around here really that bad?"

Alexis laughed. "Most people think so. I think it's fine. If you don't like the weather in Wisconsin, I always tell people to move. I like having four seasons. It's long, though. Everything goes gray and dead around here, and you basically won't see any warmth until maybe April. And even then, it's not for long. As long as you're in school, once fall hits, it'll simply be cold."

Every once in a while, Vickie looked up from the ground to see other kids chuckling at her or whispering while they stared at her. A few even pointed.

Her companion tilted her head to see her watching the others snicker. "Are you sure you're okay?" She nudged her with her elbow. "Hey. Are you more embarrassed than you let on?"

The vampire shook her head. "I'm not embarrassed, but I am angry. Every time I see Megan in class, I want to tackle her and make her regret it."

Alexis smirked. "You're probably not the only one in our school to feel that way. But Megan thinks she's untouchable. She's gotten away with so much over the years that nobody will challenge her."

"Yeah, well, that's not how I work."

"Hey, girls."

They both looked to their right to see a pack of boys running past. In the middle the group, Eric waved wildly with a big smile on his face. They grinned and returned the greeting, and he disappeared into the distance.

"I don't care what other people think. All these kids can talk, but it doesn't matter to me."

"It should."

"I thought you told me to not be embarrassed by it and let it go. How can it also matter to me what they think if I'm supposed to ignore this?"

"What I mean is don't let it consume you. But you should pay attention to your reputation. That's different than letting yourself be a victim to all of this." Alexis uncrossed her legs and leaned forward to talk a little quieter. "Kids in high school are relentless. Once you have a reputation, they'll hammer you about it for the next few years. And if you show you are bothered by it, they'll hit you even harder. What you need to do is overcome that reputation and change their minds. Otherwise, you'll be haunted by this until graduation."

Vickie twisted her face in confusion. "Why would they be so relentless about something so stupid?"

"Because teenagers are stupid." Alexis sighed. "They suck. All of them. They pick the dumbest things to concern themselves with. Stupid. Plain and simple."

"So there's no way around this? I'm stuck with these people until I graduate?"

"It almost makes you miss hiding in a box, doesn't it?"

"Let's not go that far." The two girls laughed.

"What happened in the old days? When you were back

home, how did other kids react when you embarrassed yourself?"

Vickie scanned her memory but came up with nothing. "I don't ever remember being embarrassed back home."

"Ever?"

"Ever. I was scared sometimes. Being a vampire puts you on alert, we've talked about that. Angry. Nervous once in a while. But never really embarrassed. We never cared what other people thought about us. And they obviously couldn't record you and send it to hundreds of people at a time. So we merely cared about ourselves, not other people."

"Wait, that's not true," Alexis said. "You cared. Your dad insisted you couldn't use your powers around people in the town because of what they would think, right?"

Vickie looked at her with raised eyebrows. "That's not because he was worried they'd make fun of me. It's because he was worried they would cut my head off." Alexis looked away for a moment. "We made our decisions based on what people did, not what they thought."

"Sorry. I didn't mean to bring it up."

"It's fine."

"Other girls have embarrassed me before." Alexis had an understanding tone in her voice and tried to show a little empathy.

"Oh yeah, Megan with the face bruise, right?"

"Well, yeah, but that's not the one I was thinking of. That one embarrassed me because I love Christmas. There was a time when girls really humiliated me in front of my classmates."

Vickie leaned back to rest against the backrest of the

bench. The warmth of the metal baking in the sunshine sent a wave of pleasure down her spine. "What happened?"

Alexis folded her hands in her lap and toyed with a ring on her right hand. "A bunch of jerk girls gave me a bubbler ride."

"What's a bubbler ride?"

"A bubbler is a water fountain. That's what we call it around here." She smirked as she'd forgotten that people outside of Wisconsin didn't know what a bubbler was. "A bubbler ride is when they sit you on the water fountain and turn the water on. It gets your pants wet, especially on the crotch."

Vickie shook her head in undisguised confusion. "Why?"

"Because they think it's funny. Actually, I was a special case. Normally, girls don't give bubbler rides. That's the kind of thing boys do. Every boy who's played a sport at this high school has had a bubbler ride at some point. It's part of initiation."

"But what makes it so funny? So your pants are wet. What's the point?"

"When the crotch of your pants is wet, it looks like you peed yourself." Alexis stared off into the distance and thought about that fateful day. "They did it to me right before the last period of the day. The whole class stared when I walked in with my wet pants."

"Did they laugh at you?"

"Oh geez, yeah. They laughed a lot. Pointed, laughed, giggled, talked...it was something I lived down for, like, an entire week. And there was a cute boy in that class I had tried to get closer to. That didn't happen, obviously."

"Why would they laugh?" She still had trouble understanding the point of the joke. "Everyone knew it was only water."

"It doesn't matter. The only thing that matters in high school is how something looks. They thought it looked like I peed, so that's what they laughed about." She looked at her watch. "My dad will be here soon. Let's start walking."

Craig picked the girls up every day in front of the football field. It was about a block away from the entrance to the school, but it allowed them to avoid the bottleneck of traffic at the front of the building. He could pick them up, make a quick U-turn, and be back on the freeway headed home right away.

As they walked down the sidewalk, a few more kids pointed and smirked at Vickie.

"Let me get this straight. All that happened was I was asked out on a joke date by a popular guy who had no intention of dating me. I was one hundred percent the victim here, but because I looked like a loser when it happened, they'll treat me like a loser?"

"Exactly like the bubbler ride." Alexis nodded sadly. "All that happened was a few girls sat me on the water fountain and turned the water on. I was totally the victim, but because my pants looked like I'd wet myself, they treated me like a loser."

There was a brief silence. "Teenagers really are stupid," Vickie said quietly and actually winced at the thought.

"They sure are."

They stopped in front of the usual pickup place. Through the bars of the fence, the girls watched the football team conduct their warmup drills. Dozens of older boys in full pads ran in place, did pushups, and shouted at each other. Leading the pack was Steve Miick.

"They sure are intense." Vickie grabbed the bars of the fence and rested her head on them.

"That's football. You gotta be tough or something. I don't really get it. But they scream a lot."

"And they run around hitting each other? Tackling each other?"

"Yep."

Vickie thought about her speed and strength. "That could be fun."

Alexis burst out laughing. "What, now you want to join the football team?"

"Why not? I'm faster than any of them. I'm stronger, too. I bet I could whip all of them in football."

The other girl patted her on the back. "Oh, I have no doubt you would. And I would pay good money to watch that happen. Football jocks are some of the biggest idiots on the planet. It would be hilarious to watch them be put in their place by a girl. But they don't allow girls on the team. And you have to try out, which you can't do anymore."

Vickie pursed her lips. "What if I simply ran out there now and knocked them all over?" A devilish smile spread across her face.

"Oh, man." Alexis put her hands on her hips. "Can you imagine?"

"I'd probably start with Steve. Send him flying. That would cut him down a few pegs."

"Now, you want to talk about embarrassment? Vickie, if you got on that field and tackled him, he would be so embarrassed, he would never recover." She laughed at the thought.

Vickie laughed at first, then stopped. "I don't know if I would want to do that, anyway. Stooping to their level? It seems... I don't know."

"You'd be suspended, for sure. Maybe we come up with a way of embarrassing them that doesn't put you at risk for punishment."

The two of them stood and watched the team warm up and eventually split into separate groups to run drills. Steve dodged and darted his way around cones and through tackling dummies. It was impressive—to Alexis, at least.

"That boy is strong and fast."

"Not like me."

"No, not like you. This is one of those times where I wish you didn't have to hide your powers. Even simply running out on that field and being faster than him would humiliate him so badly."

Vickie released the bars of the fence and looked at Alexis. "I'll do something. I don't know what yet. But if everyone cares so much about what people think, then it will be my turn to make sure everyone thinks they suck. Or at least Megan."

"Don't get yourself suspended, okay? You're still the new girl here. Don't get that reputation."

The vampire made no response and merely continued to daydream about embarrassing Steve. Minutes later, Craig pulled up in the SUV.

"There's my dad. Let's go." They crawled into the back of the vehicle.

"Hey, girls. How was school today?"

"It was fine," Vickie replied, even though it was a lie she couldn't remotely believe.

Alexis smiled. With only three words, Vickie had begun to act more and more like a regular teenager.

CHAPTER FOURTEEN

It was a Sunday afternoon. Craig had spent the last several hours in his recliner watching football on the TV.

The girls had volunteered to make dinner. Alexis pulled out a premade pizza crust from the kitchen cabinet. "This will be good stuff and a nice way for you to get used to cooking in this house. Pizza is fairly easy to make, and it's perfect football food."

Vickie sat on a stool at the kitchen counter. "Football food? What do you mean?"

"There are certain kinds of snacks and food that go well with watching a Packer game. Easy stuff. Food you can eat with your fingers, usually. Except for chili, which is a football food you eat with a spoon, but we'll get to that eventually." She crossed to the oven and set it to preheat. "If you watch the Packers, you want pretzels, cheese dip, maybe chips. You can eat burgers if you want, but pizza is always a great way to go."

"There are so many rules in your society." Vickie folded

her arms and rested them on the counter. "Why is that? You can only eat certain foods at certain times and on certain days?"

Alexis pulled out a jar of pizza sauce. "It's not a rule. It's simply understood. For the Packer experience, you want certain kinds of foods."

The vampire unwrapped the pizza crust and placed it on the counter. Alexis used a spoon to dump the jar of sauce onto the crust and spread it out to the edges.

"Hey, so…those guys running past us after school with Eric?"

"The cross country team?"

"That's the cross country team. Okay." Vickie nodded. "I thought so, but I wasn't sure. I knew that Eric was on the team, but I didn't know what they looked like."

Alexis gave her a funny look while she pulled cheese and pepperoni out of the fridge. "Why do you care what they look like?"

"I don't mean it like that. I simply didn't know what cross country looked like."

"Basically, like that. Running. And lots of it."

"I thought about joining."

Alexis set the pepperoni and the package of cheese on the counter and leaned one hand on it as she turned to look at her. "You want to join the cross country team? Now? They're well into the season."

"Do you think I could join this team?"

The other girl tore open the bag of cheese and handed it to her. "You probably could. It's a no-cut team."

"What does that mean?"

"It means they don't really have tryouts. If you want to

be a runner, you get to be a runner. With other sports, you have to try out and they make sure you're good enough to be on the team. Cross country doesn't attract very many people, so they don't have cuts."

"That's good, right?" Vickie took a handful from the bag of cheese and sprinkled it on the sauced crust. "That means I should be able to be on the team if I ask. I am a little worried, though."

"About what?"

"Puking."

Alexis tilted her head and squinted at her. "Puking? That's what you're worried about?"

She continued to add the cheese carefully. "Eric talked a lot about runners throwing up after big workouts or something like that. He talked about it a lot."

"That doesn't happen as often as he says. At least, not to the girls. I don't think so, anyway. I feel that if puking was such a regular occurrence, we'd all hear about it more. If they let you join the team, you'll have practices, workouts, and stuff like that. Then I think you race maybe once a week."

"I can handle that, right?" She finished covering the crust.

Alexis grabbed a handful of pepperoni and scattered the pieces carefully across the bed of cheese. "I guess. Do you really want to, though? Don't you want to do something…I don't know, safer? You could jump into music. I'll be there and I can help guide you through it."

"Eric will be there. He'll look out for me."

"He is on the boys' team." Her sister shook her head. "They do different things. He wouldn't run beside you.

Didn't you notice that he only ran with boys when they passed us the today?"

I didn't think of that. I wouldn't be running side by side with Eric. I'd be running with the girls. Still, I would be closer to him, right?

Alexis slid the pizza into the heated oven and set the timer. She tossed Vickie a rag and asked her to wipe the counter. "See? Not so hard. Cooking can be easy."

"That was fine." She wiped the sauce drips off the countertop. "I still want to try the cross country team, though. Even if I don't run with Eric. I think it would be good for me to try something. And the worst they can do is tell me no, so it's not like I would risk much."

A cheer rang out from the living room.

"The Packer game must be on." Alexis laughed. "Dad really gets into these games. I'm warning you now, he'll get loud. Try not to talk to him until there's a commercial on."

The two girls walked into the living room as he leapt to his feet and pumped his fist. "Woo-hoo! First touchdown of the season, girls." He raised his open hand. Vickie flinched, ready to protect herself from a slap.

Alexis gave him a high five. Once the vampire realized this, she joined in but remained a little confused.

The savory aroma of melting cheese filled the house while the Packers kicked an extra point and Craig clapped his hands. "The road to the Super Bowl begins today."

Vickie's eyes widened to see so much volume and energy coming from the mild-mannered man who had previously sat in that chair.

"I told you." Alexis laughed. "It's not only him. The Packers bring it out in everybody. It's how fans are."

The game went to a commercial, and Vickie turned to him. "Can I ask you a question?"

"Fire away."

"Can I join the cross country team?"

He raised his eyebrows in surprise. Alexis watched his reaction closely. "Do you think you can handle it?"

"The running?" She giggled. "Yeah, I think I can handle it."

"No, that's not what I mean. I wonder if you can handle being around so many other kids in such a close-knit situation." She frowned a little, bewildered by what he meant. "Being in a sport is a great thing. But you do have to remember that you'll be surrounded by other kids for long stretches of time. On your own, too. Alexis won't be there to help you out. There will be times when you'll be on overnight trips and will have to sleep around others. You'll have to change in the locker room with them. These aren't bad things, they're merely… They're times when you will be vulnerable. Let's put it that way."

The commercial break ended, and he paused the conversation to watch the game. The hated Chicago Bears marched the ball down the field but were stopped short. "All right. Force a field goal." Craig clapped his hands again. "You can't win this game with only field goals, boys."

Another commercial break started, and Craig turned to continue the conversation. Alexis piped in first with a smile. "I think she only wanted to be near Eric."

Vickie shrugged and nodded. "I like Eric. I think he's cute. I'm not embarrassed by that."

Craig's stomach knotted a little when he thought about guiding this girl through dating. "He would be embarrassed by it, so tread carefully there. Is that the only reason you want to join cross country?"

She looked out the window at the gray afternoon. The wind knocked a few leaves off the tree in the front yard and the gray clouds gave her a weird sense of homesickness. Most days were gray in Salzburg. "I simply want to do something. I want to be myself in a way. Most of the time, at school, I'm only Alexis' cousin or I'm the weird foreign kid. I want to establish my own reputation."

Craig nodded. "I know what you mean." They paused again for another drive by the Packers, which was stopped short. As they punted the ball away, he shook his head. At the commercial, he resumed the discussion. "You know, when I was in high school, I was on the football team."

"Really? Is that why you're such a fan of the Green Bay Packers?" Vickie asked innocently.

"No, I was a fan long before that. Like any good father, my dad raised me with green and gold in my blood. You don't have to play football to watch football. No, I was a wide receiver in high school. That meant I caught passes from the quarterback—the guy throwing the ball."

"And did you like it?"

"I loved it. I made friends and bonded with my teammates. Nothing brings a group of kids together like adversity and physical challenge. When you have to work your tails off together, you develop a close connection. I don't know how it is in cross country—we called them field fairies back then. It was a different time. But I know they work hard, and I would imagine they bond over tough workouts and long runs together."

"Did you ever puke?"

Craig curled his lip up. "Why?"

"Eric talked a lot about puking, apparently," Alexis said with an annoyed tone in her voice. "He told her they run so hard they throw up. He must have talked about it a lot because that's all she seemed to take away from the conversation."

"I threw up a couple of times. But that's not the point. The point is, we worked hard together, and we all grew together. That could be worthwhile for you."

"That happens in the music department, too," Alexis said and lowered her voice to speak to Vickie while the game resumed. "We spend a lot of time in practices and rehearsals, especially around concert season. You put in so many extra hours together, you bond. Friendships really grow strong. That's why I'm so close to Jess and Jamie. We've spent so much time together working hard and practicing. It's different from sports, but it's the same kind of thing."

The timer went off on the oven and the two girls returned to the kitchen to examine their handiwork. Alexis pulled the oven door open to reveal a perfectly baked pizza with a deliciously browned crust and bubbling mozzarella cheese on top. She slid it onto a baking sheet and put it on the counter to slice.

"It smells really good." Vickie smiled. "I hope it tastes good."

"It will. Pizza is hard to screw up."

They cut off a couple of slices and put them on a plate. Vickie took it into the living room and handed it to Craig. He picked up a slice and took a bite. "Delicious. See, you're getting the hang of this stuff. Nice work and thank you for helping to make dinner." She smiled proudly. "Listen, Vickie, if you want to try a sport, you have our full support. We want you to try stuff and learn more. If that will make you happy, give it a go and we'll see what happens with it."

She smiled quietly as she walked out of the room. *I get to meet a few new people, work on my reputation as more than simply the foreign girl, and maybe even get a little closer to Eric. This could be really good for me.*

A little excited, she served a few slices of pizza for herself and returned to the living room. It was time to learn more about the Packers, and Craig was more than willing to teach her.

CHAPTER FIFTEEN

"We have time this morning," Alexis said. "This is your best chance to talk to Mr. Lueck. Let's go find him."

The two girls walked down the early-morning hallways toward the Social Studies Hall of the school building. Mr. Lueck taught several history classes, and he was in his classroom prepping for the day when the girls knocked on his door.

He looked up from his desk and waved them in politely. The teacher was built like a lifelong distance runner with a thin upper torso and muscular legs. His skin, tanned from putting in the miles outside, made his bright blue eyes seem to pop. The long black hair that waved down his neck was a remnant from his years of running for the high school as a member of the team in the 1980s.

Lueck spoke with a happy, sing-song tone in his voice. "Good morning, girls. What can I do for you today?"

Alexis nudged Vickie with her elbow to remind her to speak.

"Oh." She shook off the mental cobwebs. "I wondered if I could be on the cross country team."

He raised his eyebrows. "Well, that's wonderful. I'm always happy to welcome new team members. Believe it or not, cross country is not the most popular sport here in the school." He flashed a self-deprecating smile. "But it really isn't that easy. We have our first meet on Friday night." He gritted his teeth. "So…I want you to be on the team. But can you be ready by then? What kind of running experience do you have? Any?"

Vickie nodded. "I've run my whole life."

Alexis fought off a smile. *The two of them are having completely different conversations.*

Mr. Lueck leaned back in his desk chair, folded his hands with his index fingers pointing up, and touched them to his lip as he thought for a moment. "I'll tell you what," he said and pointed both fingers at Vickie. "Let's get you out on the track and run a quick mile. I want to see where you are, ability-wise. If you can cut a decent time, maybe I'll feel a little better about you keeping up with the rest of the team. How about at lunch today? I'm off both lunch periods."

Vickie looked at Alexis, who nodded her approval. "Okay."

"And your name is?"

"Oh, I'm Vickie Hewitt." They shook hands. "Thank you for the opportunity."

"Of course." He smiled. "I'll be out on the track with my stopwatch. And let me quickly write you a pass to get out there. Otherwise, they won't let you leave the building during school hours."

Alexis raised a finger. "Mr. Lueck? I have second lunch, but Vickie has first lunch. I hoped to at least be out there for moral support. You know, this is her first big tryout for anything here in America. I want to be able to be there to cheer her on."

He smiled warmly. "I love to see that. I'll write you a pass, too." He winked at her. "Even if you are using this to get out of whatever class you have during first lunch. It's not a history class, is it?"

"Nope."

"Then it's fine by me." He laughed and handed the passes to the girls.

They thanked him and left the room. Vickie hopped in place with excitement. "I get to try out for a sport."

"You'll do great."

"And that's so nice of you to want to be there to support me."

"Sisters gotta watch out for each other."

As they walked, Alexis smiled quietly. That wasn't why she was going out there with her. *If she runs too fast, she'll stand out like a sore thumb. I'll watch Lueck's reactions and see if I can help her keep her speed under control. I don't want her getting too excited and accidentally setting a world record for the mile.*

Once the lunch hour arrived, the girls met at the back door of the building. Vickie peeked through the window of the door and saw Mr. Lueck walk along the track with a stopwatch hung around his neck.

"Are you nervous?" Alexis asked with a smile.

"A little. I don't know why. I can run fine."

"It's because it's new. Don't worry, I've got your back on

this one. Go out there and— Well, don't do your best. If you run too fast, you'll cause a stir. Try to pace yourself a little."

They walked across the parking lot to the football field and track, where the coach waited with a smile on his face. It fell as soon as he saw them.

"Um, Vickie?" He pointed to her clothes. "Do you plan to run in that?" She wore a pair of jeans and a long-sleeved t-shirt with sneakers. "That's not really running gear."

"I don't have running gear. But if I make the team, I'll get some. I promise."

He shrugged his shoulders. "Okay…well, here we go, then. Over here is the starting line. I want you to run a mile, and I'll clock you to see how fast you go. A mile is four laps around the track, got it?"

"Got it."

Alexis clapped as the vampire stepped up to the starting line. "Go get it, girl."

Lueck raised his stopwatch. "On your mark…get set… go." He started his stopwatch with a beep and Vickie broke into a run down the track.

She increased her pace and her legs pumped quickly. Alexis watched with concern. *That might be too fast, Vickie. Shoot. Ease up a little.*

As the vampire crossed the first two-hundred-meter point, Coach Lueck's eyes widened. "Good grief."

"What is it?"

"She's running at, like, a world record pace. That can't be right."

"Let her keep going. I'll cheer her on from the other side." Alexis jogged off to the other side of the track.

Vickie crossed the starting line and completed her first lap. "Nice work, Vickie. Keep it up," the teacher shouted, still concerned about the time on his stopwatch. "This is impossible."

As she reached the other side of the track, Alexis jogged up to her and tried to talk to her without the man hearing her. "Vickie, slow down. You're going too fast. It's drawing too much attention so ease up."

Vickie nodded and slowed down considerably. Coach Lueck nodded as he watched the time while she crossed the halfway point. "Settle into a pace, Vickie. You're doing great."

After the final two laps were finished, the vampire crossed the finish line and he clapped. Alexis jogged to meet her and threw her arm around her shoulder. "Look tired," she whispered.

"What?"

"Heavy breathing. Pretend this was hard for you. Don't look normal. Look like this was a lot of work."

She forced herself to breathe heavily, clutched her chest, and pretended to get her breathing under control.

"That was really impressive, Vickie." Lueck looked at his stopwatch. "Here's the thing—you started out really fast. Like, way too fast. Your mile clocked in at five minutes, thirty-two seconds."

"Is that good?"

"That's great. It's a varsity-level mile so I love it. But a race is not a mile. It's a five-K, so that's 3.1 miles. What looked like happened here is you went out way too strongly, and you ran out of steam as the mile wore on. If this were a race, you'd only be a third of the way through it. You'd burn out of the race before the halfway point."

Alexis was nervous about the tone of his voice. "I think she went out so fast because she wanted to impress you." She patted Vickie on the back to encourage her to nod agreement. "She wanted to do the fastest mile she could because she wanted to make the team, that's all."

Lueck looked at Vickie and how she "got control of her breathing" and calmed herself. "Vickie, pushing yourself is a big part of cross country running so I love that you do that. I wish all my runners challenged themselves as hard as you did now. But the other key is to pace yourself. You have to listen to your body and adjust accordingly. It's about learning when to preserve your energy and when to unleash it."

There was more silence as the wind howled. Lueck sighed inwardly while he stared at his clipboard.

"Still…if you can learn to pace yourself with the other girls, I could turn you into one heck of a runner. This kind of raw ability doesn't come along very often."

Alexis leaned in. "Are you saying she's on the team?"

He nodded. "I'm saying she's on the team."

The girls cheered and high-fived each other. Ever since Vickie had learned the high-five during the Packer game, she enjoyed any excuse to use it.

"Vickie, we practice right after school every day. I'll give you until tomorrow to get some running gear. We'll call this one practice for today. Get proper running shoes and at least wear a t-shirt and shorts, okay?"

They shook hands and returned as a group to the school building.

"That is some really raw talent you have there, Vickie. I'm looking forward to coaching you. If we can develop this ability, you could be someone I can build a winning team around." Coach Lueck seemed more excited about having her on the team with every step he took.

Once they were inside, there were a few more minutes before the bell rang. Alexis grabbed Vickie and pulled her into a side hallway. The vampire wore a smile that she couldn't wipe off her face.

"I'm going to be an athlete. This is so cool."

Alexis grinned. "It's awesome. But I do need you to be careful about pacing yourself."

"I didn't know. It's hard to feel how fast I'm going."

"It's fine, we worked our way around that. But here's what'll happen. We'll take you shopping tonight and load you up with running gear. When you get to practice tomorrow, stay near the back of the pack. Let yourself get a feel for the pace. They will do that for you. Keep up with the girls, don't lead them. Pay close attention and you will notice what they're looking for. Blend in."

The bell rang and the girls exchanged smiles and a quick hug before they went their separate ways. Vickie walked past the doors leading to the cafeteria. Eric and Jess exited and immediately looked confused when they saw her.

"Hey, where were you?" Jess asked. "We missed you at lunch today."

Vickie gave Eric a smile. "I was outside making the cross country team."

His eyebrows raised. "Really? You're running cross country now?"

She nodded excitedly. "I ran a mile for Coach Lueck and he welcomed me onto the team. I start tomorrow." She ran off to reach her next class.

Eric smiled surreptitiously. *Wow. I'll see her a lot more, then. Awesome. I hope.*

CHAPTER SIXTEEN

While Vickie was attending her first cross country practice the next day, Alexis sat outside the school on her own.

To her surprise, she felt alone.

Come on. You've sat out here by yourself how many times? Vickie has only been going to school with you for a few weeks. How quickly do you get used to something?

She sat on the bench and the cold metal sent shivers through her legs. Across the street, she saw a pack of girls from school running together. Vickie ran at the back of the group. She was calm and wide-eyed and obviously paid close attention to how fast she moved.

Alexis smiled. *I'm proud of her. She's really trying out there. And it looks like she's getting the hang of it, too. I bet she wishes she could leave them all in her dust, though.*

When Vickie disappeared around a corner, her smile dropped. She stood and walked down the sidewalk to the pickup spot to wait for her dad. A few minutes later, he pulled up and she climbed into the car.

"Hey, sweetie. How was your day?"

"It was fine." The universal exchange between a high school girl and her father.

"Weird not having Vickie waiting with you, huh?"

"Yeah."

The rest of the drive home was quiet. Whenever her father asked a question or made a comment, he received one-word replies, shrugs, and half-chuckles.

Craig wasn't stupid. He could tell something was on his daughter's mind. But he didn't want to pry and simply hoped she would get over it by the time they got home.

However, the silent treatment continued after they walked inside. He returned to his room to do a little work, and she grabbed a magazine and sat on the couch.

At his desk, he couldn't shake the feeling that he should talk to his daughter. He looked at the photo of Carol on the wall. *You would march right up to her and talk to her, wouldn't you? You'd ask her what's wrong, and she'd open up. I don't know if she'd open up to me like that. Even though I'm all she has, we've never gotten terribly deep together.*

He closed his eyes. *But we'll have to, won't we?*

His mind made up, he stood from his desk and walked to the living room, where he sat beside Alexis.

"What's up, Dad?"

"Are you okay?"

"Sure, I'm fine." She wanted to end it there, but he stared at her in silence and simply waited for her to admit the truth. "Okay, I'm not fine."

"What's bugging you? Is it that Vickie is on the cross country team now?"

"I don't know." She closed the magazine and tossed it

onto the couch with a gesture of frustration. "Okay… I'm not mad at her for being on the team. I don't resent her for being on the team. I love that she's taking such a step forward. It's good for her. And it's good for all of us too. If she were to latch onto me all the time, I'd probably be annoyed with her, wouldn't I?"

"Oh yeah." Her father laughed. "Her being on the team is great if you're talking about that. And she isn't the only one who needs independence here. You need a break from her, too."

"Right. So why does this bother me? All I can think about is whether or not she's doing okay, and if she's fitting in…" She trailed off and shrugged helplessly.

Her father smiled and put his arm around her. "You're worried about her. She's out there by herself without your protection. The truth is that she's never been out in the world without you helping her along. Now, she has to sink or swim. It's tough to watch and not be able to do anything about it."

Alexis leaned her head back against her dad's arm. "This sucks."

He burst out laughing. "You bet it sucks. But Vickie is strong, and Eric's there to keep an eye on her, just in case. She'll figure it out. You did."

She pulled her eyebrows together and looked at him. "What do you mean?"

"Oh please," he said. "I don't think I slept the whole first week you were in high school. You were out of the nest and away from our protection. I was worried sick. Would the other girls make fun of you? Would boys not like you? Or would they like you too much? Would you be able to keep up with your classes? Would you make friends, or would you be the weird kid with no friends? There are a million reasons why a father would worry about his daughter going to high school. And I had them all."

She smiled. "Did Mom worry about me?"

He looked across the room at the family picture on the bookshelf. "Yeah. We both did. I think she tried to play it cool, though. I'd look over to see if she was awake in the middle of the night like I was so I could pester her. But she'd be sleeping every time. I think she was actually awake and pretending to sleep because she didn't want to talk about it."

"That sounds like Mom." Alexis laughed and a wistful tone crept into her voice. "She was stubborn about the cancer, so I bet she was stubborn about that too."

"You're not kidding." Craig smiled when he thought about his wife. "You know, high school wasn't the first time we freaked out about you, either."

"No?"

He shook his head. "Kindergarten was way worse."

Alexis sat up and looked at him with her jaw agape. "Kindergarten? Seriously?"

"Oh, you have no idea."

"What's so scary about kindergarten?"

"Lex, kindergarten is the start."

"Of what?"

"Everything. For five full years, we had you all to ourselves. If we were home, so were you. I came home every day, and you were there. Your mom was home during the day, and you were with her. We knew where you were and what you were doing at all times."

"So when I started kindergarten, that was the first time I was really away from you guys."

He nodded. "Not only that, but it was the start of you being away from us forever. Being a parent is a tough job. We're supposed to take care of you, but the biggest job we have is teaching you to not need us. If you grow up and you're still dependent on your parents for everything, the parents screwed up somewhere. You going to kindergarten was the first test of all that. It's bittersweet because it's the start of twenty years of you going out on your own, progressively getting more and more independent."

"Maybe that's how I feel with Vickie." Alexis looked out the window. "I want her to be independent, but I like teaching her stuff. Now, she's out by herself and I wonder what'll happen to her. And I've only known her a little while. Is this what parenting feels like?"

"Times a billion."

"What calmed you down? How did you get over it and let me go?"

Her father laughed. "Well, first of all, the law said you had to go. It didn't matter if we felt ready or not. We had no choice. But there was a point where your mom sat me down and gave me a little speech. I'll never forget what she said."

"What did she say?" Alexis leaned forward with genuine interest and anticipation. She was always eager to hear stories of her mother.

"She said, 'We raised her right.' It was such a simple little message, but it was the right thing for me to hear."

"That's it?"

"That's it. It was merely a reminder that we did the job.

We took care of you, and we prepared you for it. You're a strong girl. You knew what you were doing. And you know what? Vickie's a strong girl, too."

"Did Mom always know the right thing to say?"

"Boy, did she ever." He laughed. "There was never a point in time where she didn't know exactly what to say to keep me calm or give me confidence. She had a knack for it. Shoot, every time I have to talk to you about something, I keep asking myself, 'What would Carol say to her?' That seems to help me."

She leaned back again to rest her head on his arm. "So you think Vickie will be okay?"

"Please. She learned from the best. You've done an awesome job teaching her and taking care of her. But just like when we sent you off to kindergarten, or when we drove you to high school for the first time, there comes a point when you've taught them all you can, and the rest of their education comes from experience. She has to learn on her own like you learned on your own."

"But what if she falls on her face?"

"She will." He looked at the ceiling, his expression thoughtful. "You know, in my first football practice, we ran a scrimmage. That's when you play a fake game, right? It doesn't count for anything and you're only trying to see where everyone's skill levels are. I'm a wide receiver, and I catch a bomb pass. It was a beautiful catch. I thought for sure I had locked myself in as a starter for the team. Then I took a huge hit."

"Did you get hurt?"

"Nope. Worse. I was jarred off course and spun around. I lost my sense of direction and ran in for a touchdown…

the wrong way. I turned to do a little trash talking—as we football players tend to do—and they were all laughing at me. I was so embarrassed, I didn't even remove my helmet for the rest of practice. I didn't want anyone to see how red I was or the tears in my eyes."

"Did Grandma and Grandpa help you through it?"

"No. I didn't tell them. I suffered quietly, told them I was tired from practice, and stayed in my room all night."

Alexis sighed. "How did you get over it?"

He smiled. "I realized that these guys would hound me every day unless I did something about it. So the next scrimmage, everyone gives me grief. I caught a pass, reached into my pocket, and pulled out a compass. I stared at it as I ran down the field as a joke."

"Did they laugh?"

"Yeah. But at least they were laughing with me. I earned a lot of points with the team that day, and I saved face from then on. See, Grandma and Grandpa raised me right. I figured it out. You figured it out. And Vickie will figure it out too."

"So Mom was right."

"Of course. We can't hold Vickie's hand forever."

There was a beat of silence as the two of them stared at the picture on the bookshelf.

"I miss Mom."

"I miss her too, babe. I miss her too."

CHAPTER SEVENTEEN

Vickie walked into Coach Lueck's classroom with her bag, expecting to see a group of other runners. But she was the only one, and she paused hesitantly in the doorway.

He stood from his desk sporting a sweatshirt and a pair of running shorts. "Vickie. Glad you made it. Everyone else is getting changed, so why don't you head to the girls' locker room across the hall? Change into your running stuff and come back here. We'll get you set up from there."

She nodded. *The locker room? So I guess I have to change in front of a group of other girls? Try not to screw this up, Vickie. You can do this.*

Cautiously, she crossed the hall and pulled open the door to the locker room. She stepped around the corner and froze at the sight of about a dozen girls, all in different states of undress. They turned to look at her as she stood there, confused.

"Are you lost?" one girl asked.

"I'm…um, I'm on the cross country team."

A few girls exchanged glances as they tried to figure out what was going on. One girl pulled a sweatshirt on and walked up to her. "You're the new girl in class, right?"

She nodded. "I'm Vickie."

"I'm Krista. Nice to meet you." She gave her a warm smile, which melted away some of the uncertainty. "Do you know what you're doing?"

"I'm supposed to get changed into my running gear." She held her bag out.

"Yep. Do you have a locker in here?" When she received no response, she shrugged. "Okay, that's fine. I tell you what, you can share my locker today. Tomorrow, bring a padlock so you can have your own locker. Hey, girls. This is Vickie. She's running with us today. Be nice."

Vickie was fairly taken aback by how nice Krista was to her. She changed quickly into her running gear and slipped on her running shoes. The other girls paid no attention to her changing, much to her relief.

The vampire watched Krista gather her long, thick brown hair into a ponytail. She was a beautiful young girl of Puerto Rican descent and had a slightly high-pitched voice that made it sound like she was singing whenever she talked.

"I've seen you around school," she told Vickie. "How do you like Clear Lake so far?"

"It's fine," Vickie answered awkwardly. "I'm still a little shy, I guess."

"Well, you'll get over that quickly here." Krista laughed. "We're all sisters on this team. Follow our lead. I'll make sure you know where to go."

Once she was done changing, Vickie shut the locker

door and Krista padlocked it. They all walked back across the hall to where a few of the boys were already waiting in the classroom. Most sat at desks or on the floor. Vickie chose a desk and waited nervously for practice to start.

"We're waiting on a few more," Coach Lueck said as he scanned the room.

Eric walked in and waved at Vickie with a smile. She waved back and exhaled with relief. *It feels good to see a familiar face, at least.*

"Okay, everybody's here," the coach announced. "Before we get started, I'd like everyone to welcome Vickie Hewitt to the team. Be nice to her." He laughed. "Vickie is new to Clear Lake, but she seems to be a very strong runner. I look forward to seeing if we can mold her into a champion. Vickie, is there anything you'd like to say?" She shook her head and slunk lower in her seat. "I tell you what, why don't you simply say something interesting about yourself? We're all friends here."

Her stomach dropped. *I thought I was done with this say something interesting stuff after the first week of school. I should simply say I'm a vampire and see if they all freak out.*

"I'm from Austria—Salzburg, actually. I've lived in America for a while now and I really like it."

"What's your favorite part of living in Milwaukee?" Lueck asked.

"Um…probably Summerfest. That was a lot of fun. The music, the crowds, the food. That was great. We didn't have anything like that where I come from."

"Awesome. Well, thanks for joining us, Vickie. I'm sure you'll fit in great." She sat as the coach continued and paced at the front of the room as he spoke. "Now, this

Friday is our first meet at McCarty Park. I'm still finalizing team lineups—who's in Varsity and who's in JV. So stay tuned there. For those who are new to the team this year, meet weeks are usually a little lighter, so that's probably why Vickie waited until now to start." The group chuckled. "We don't want to wear ourselves out with any hard workouts and risk running out of gas by Friday."

"No puking today?" one of the guys shouted with a laugh.

"No puking today, Sonnenburg," the coach said. "But wait until next week. I have a killer lined up." Everyone laughed.

Vickie failed to see the humor. *Again with the puking. What is it with everyone and throwing up?*

"Because we'll go lighter today, I want both teams to stay together. No splitting into Varsity and JV or anything like that. This is a good chance for everyone to run together and be a team. Guys, I want you to go out for an easy six miles today. Girls, let's do five miles."

Five miles? Vickie tried to keep herself from reacting as nobody else seemed phased by this information. *I thought we only ran three miles. How am I supposed to keep pretending I'm slow for five miles?*

The coach dismissed them and the girls gathered outside the door. A tall, skinny blonde girl seemed to lead the whole group. "All right, girls," she said, "let's go out the side door. We'll circle around the school and go down Bluemound Avenue, then head to LaFollette Park."

The girls walked toward the door but Krista hung back to walk with Vickie. "That's Shannon. She's the team captain." The vampire nodded. "Follow our lead and you'll do fine. We all have to stay together today. Are you sure you can keep up with us?"

She smiled. "I'm sure I'll be fine."

Once out the door, dozens of watches beeped as all the girls started the timers and set off. *Shoot, I don't have a watch. Should I have a watch? Will I look stupid for asking? Don't overthink this, just ask.*

"Hey…Krista…" she stuttered. "Should I wear a watch?"

The girl smiled while they leaned into the hill leading out of the parking lot. "Yeah, you should. But that's okay. Get one by Race Day this Friday and you'll be fine."

They all huffed and puffed as they crossed the street and ran out in front of the school building. Vickie was amused by how hard everyone was breathing. *I guess I should fake this too. Boy, I wouldn't think they'd already be out of breath.*

"So, Vickie," a voice shouted from the middle of the pack. "You're the girl who was stood up at Johnny V's!"

Vickie groaned. "Yeah." *Great, I'll hear about this every day now.*

"That really sucks," the voice said. "Steve Miick is a jerk. Don't worry about him."

A few others shouted their displeasure with the situation and offered their support for her, and a feeling of warmth rushed through her. She had support from her peers, even though this was the first time they had met. It was such a simple gesture, but it meant so much to her.

"Ow."

The vampire was so moved by the support that she'd stopped paying attention to her pace. She had unknowingly increased her speed and accidentally stepped on the back of another girl's heel. Her shoe popped off and she scraped her Achilles.

"Hold up!" Shannon shouted from the front of the pack. She circled to find the girl limping off to the side. "What happened?"

"Vickie stepped on my shoe."

She grimaced and pleaded for their forgiveness, her expression one of abject repentance. "I'm so sorry. I wasn't paying attention. It won't happen again. Are you okay?"

Krista grabbed her by the shoulders and pulled her back. "Whoa, easy. Don't take it so hard. It was an accident. It happens, okay?"

Shannon nodded while the girl slipped her shoe on again and retied the laces. "But be a little more careful. That's how injuries happen, girls. You have to pay attention to what you're doing. Let's go."

She jogged to the front of the pack and everyone resumed their run with Vickie bringing up the rear.

"I'm sorry to hear about that whole Steve Miick thing," Krista puffed. "Some people in this school really suck."

Vickie laughed. "That's what Alexis says."

"Alexis Watson? How do you know her?"

"She's my cousin."

"Oh, no kidding. She's a nice girl. I don't know her that well, but she's all right. A lot of the kids suck."

"Can I ask you a question?" She felt she had a friend in the girl and could get some honest answers.

"What?"

"Do you give bubbler rides?"

Krista laughed, and a few of the other girls who overheard smiled as they ran. "Are you really worried about bubbler rides?"

"Well, yeah. Alexis got one during her freshman year. Or she says so. And she says it's more common in sports. So I figured if I'm the new girl, maybe you would wind up giving me a bubbler ride or something."

"That's a boy thing," another girl called. "Guys are idiots."

"You don't do that?"

"That's an initiation for the boys," Krista said. "Boys like to prank each other and torture each other. The only thing we do the same as the boys is taxes."

"What are taxes?"

"Taxes are for the day before Race Day, so that means it's on Thursday this week. Freshmen and newcomers to the team have to bring baked goods for everyone to eat. Sometimes, you have to carry a bag here and there. Keep your head down, bring your taxes, and we'll all get along fine."

"What kind of baked good?"

The girls all shouted suggestions.

"Cookies."

"Brownies."

"No, coffee cake."

"Coffee cake? Are you serious?"

"I love coffee cake."

"Just bring something you know is good." Krista smiled at her. "And if you have to buy something from the store, we'll overlook it this first time since you're new."

As they ran, the conversation grew quieter and less frequent. Since she'd stepped on that girl's foot, Vickie paid close attention to where she was and how everyone around her ran. She tried to emulate them as much as she could.

What ended up being the most work for her was pretending to be tired as the run stretched. The miles racked up and they didn't bother her in the least. She could hold her breath if she wanted to.

As a result, she spent most of her energy trying to look as though she was as tired as they were.

You're killing it, Vickie. Just fit in. That's all you have to do. Don't be a hero, don't try to do too much. Focus on fitting in. These are sweet girls. You'll do fine on this team.

As they approached the school building at the end of their run, she felt a little more comfortable about asking them questions. "Do we ever run with the boys?" *Maybe I can spend time running with Eric. That would be fun.*

Most of the girls curled their lips at the suggestion. Shannon stepped forward to offer a response. "The boys generally run faster than we do. Or most of them do, anyway. The girls have a different training regimen than they do, so we don't usually run with them."

"Sometimes in the summer," Krista added.

"Yeah, in the summer we do some runs together," Shannon said. "But those are basically for when we are not so worried about time and training. They're more fun runs."

Oh, well. I guess I won't run with Eric for now. That's okay, though. I just survived my first sports practice.

CHAPTER EIGHTEEN

Back at home, Craig was preparing to head out the door to pick Vickie up from her first practice.

"Do you want to come?"

"No thanks." Alexis looked up from her computer at the kitchen table. "I'll talk to her when she gets home. Besides, I can at least get dinner going while you're gone."

"Hmm. Good call."

She smiled politely at him and returned to her computer.

Craig cradled his keys in his hand and stepped away from the door. "Is everything okay? Are you still worried about Vickie? I thought we covered this."

"No, it's…something else." *Man, I wish Mom were here. It would be so much easier to talk to her.*

"You really seem down today. You're too young to carry so much on your shoulders. What is it?"

She closed her laptop. "Eric likes Vickie."

He shrugged. "Okay. So?"

"So? Come on, Dad. One of my best friends likes my new best friend? You don't see the problem there?"

"Does she like him?"

"It seems that way, yeah. She's interested if nothing else."

He laughed. "Well, I wouldn't worry too much about it. Eric is a nice boy, and Vickie is from four centuries ago. I'd say they're both a little old-fashioned."

"Dad…"

"Okay, okay. So what, are you jealous? Do you like Eric?"

"It's not that. I don't know, I just don't… Ugh!" *I don't even know how to say it.*

"Honey, why does it bother you so much? Talk to me. I'm your dad. Remember that killer advice I gave you a little while ago? Let me take another crack at it. I bet I can go two for two today and win Father of the Year. Let's do it."

She rolled her eyes. "It feels like everyone's got somebody but me, you know?"

"Well, hang on a second—"

"No, it's true. Everyone has a boyfriend or girlfriend or is interested in somebody, or whatever. And here I am, wandering around by myself with no one even remotely interested in taking me out on a date."

Craig pulled a chair up the table and looked at her for a moment. Alexis was as beautiful to him now as she had been the day she was born. She had her mother's eyes. Whenever he missed his wife, he could look at her and see her living on through her.

"You're a beautiful young girl."

"You have Dad Goggles on."

"Dad Goggles?" He laughed out loud. "What are Dad Goggles?"

"They're what they sound like. Dad Goggles—you see me as your daughter. That's all I am. So you see me like that and you think that I'm beautiful even if I'm hideous."

"If you were hideous, I'd avoid the topic." He took her hand. *Man, I wish Carol were here to help with this right now. It would be so much easier.* "Do Jess and Jamie have anybody? Are they dating right now? I haven't heard anything about them dating."

"No, but that's different. Look, it annoys me that Vickie can walk into a high school and instantly have someone crushing on her when I've been there for a lot longer and nobody seems to be interested in me."

Craig leaned back and stared out the bay window in the kitchen. *Girls are so complicated. I never worried about this stuff when I was in high school. Do they always compare themselves to each other? I don't know how to respond to this.*

He chose his next words carefully, not wanting to say the wrong thing and accidentally make the situation worse.

"When I was in high school—"

"Ugh, Dad, please don't. Not more stories from when you were a kid."

"Hey, do you want me to help or not? You're talking to me, aren't you? So listen to the story. When I was in high school, in my freshman year, I met this girl named Katie. Now Katie was a knockout. All four years of high school, she was the best-looking girl in the entire class. She was tall, blonde...had everything a guy wanted."

Alexis arched her eyebrows, knowing that was her father's way of not admitting to her that the girl had boobs.

"Now, I didn't follow her around or anything. I wasn't that kind of in love with her. But I was crazy about her. She was so cute. And sweet. That was always my thing. My class was full of good-looking people, but they were all jerks. Katie wasn't a jerk. She was the best."

"So you asked her out, or what?" Alexis tried to figure out where her father was going with this story.

"No, our paths didn't cross a whole lot. We knew each other, and we were always friendly toward each other. But we didn't hang out. We weren't in the same circles. My senior year, we did see each other a little more often, so we could still call each other friend. That was nice."

"I'm waiting to see where this is going—"

"Hang on, Miss Impatient. There's a punch line here, I promise. On the last day of school—the last day of my senior year and the last day when I would see all these classmates in one place—I passed my yearbook around school. My friends all signed it and put little messages in, jotted down memories, all that good stuff. And I remember this like it was yesterday…"

Alexis watched her father get lost in the story. It always amused her whenever he did that.

"Between third and fourth period, Katie and I traded yearbooks. I was notoriously shy and self-conscious, so this was a big deal for me. I wrote in her yearbook that I'd had a crush on her for four years. I decided that, even if I wound up embarrassed by it, maybe she would think it was funny. Worst case scenario, I'd never seen this girl again. After fourth period, we traded our yearbooks again and I ran to my next class. When I got there, I sat down, opened the yearbook, and saw what she wrote."

"What did she write?" *Darn it, he always sucks me in with these stories.*

"She wrote that she'd had a crush on me for four years."

Alexis laughed out loud. "You guys liked each other and never knew it?"

Her father nodded solemnly. "I don't know why she never admitted it. I didn't have the courage to tell her. And because of that, we both missed out on an opportunity to date each other. But that's not the point. The point is, you're at a school with over a thousand students. About half of those students are boys. In high school, many boys hide their crushes from girls because they're too shy."

He caught her eye and made sure she actually looked at him and paid attention. "Just because you don't have a date right now doesn't mean you won't ever have a date, dear. Trust me. Maybe there's a great guy out there but he's a little nervous about talking to you. Give him some time. He'll come around eventually."

She leaned back in her chair and shook her head. "How in the world do you come up with this?"

"What?" He said with a smirk as he stood up from the table.

"You have a story for everything. I'm starting to think you make these up so you have something relevant to say."

He put one hand in his pocket and flipped his keys into the air with the other. "Can I tell you a dirty little secret about your father? He used to be in high school. I know there weren't so many computers and phones, and there was no social media—thank God—but all the stuff you're going through is all the same stuff I went through when I was your age. High school is universal. Everyone goes through it. Some better than others, but we all have the same experiences to some extent."

She flipped her laptop again open. "Do you really think there's somebody out there with a crush on me who doesn't want to say it yet?"

"I'm positive. But for his sake, I hope he keeps it to himself. Because you're not dating until you're in your thirties."

"Oh, Dad."

"You laugh, but I'm serious, girl. I don't want to see any dudes sniffing around my daughter. You're all I've got now. If you thought I was overprotective before…"

She looked at him with a cocked eyebrow. He winked at her.

"I'll be back with Vickie. Keep the house from burning down, okay?"

He walked out the door and climbed into the driver's seat of the SUV. After turning the key to start the engine, he looked at the sky.

Got out of that one. You really pick the most inconvenient times to not be here, you know that, Carol? Leaving me here with a girl who's going through a crisis of romance… If she starts dating soon, you better come back here and deal with it.

Somewhere, he knew, Carol was laughing at him.

But as he drove to the school, another thought hit him. *A boy has a crush on Vickie. Hey, you know, she's basically your daughter now, too, right?*

He believed what he'd said to Alexis. Vickie was old-fashioned and with good reason, and Eric was a stand-up boy. He wasn't too worried about that.

But he also had no real experience on the female side of dating, and neither did Alexis. If Vickie and Eric were to start dating, he would have to try to help her navigate the relationship with no insight or experience that he could share.

Some days, all he had were embarrassing stories from his past. He wasn't sure that any of them would apply to this situation.

He pulled up in front of the school. Vickie exited the front doors of the building and climbed into the passenger seat with a smile on her face.

"There's my athlete. How did your first practice go? Did you make any new friends?" He stepped on the gas.

"Yeah, a few. It was nice. Plus, Eric was there, so that was good. It's always nice to see a familiar face when you're in a new place."

He kept his eyes on the road but took a deep breath. He had a feeling that, sooner or later, he would have to deal with this sort of thing. *I only hope it's later rather than sooner.*

Little did he know how much sooner it would actually be.

CHAPTER NINETEEN

After practice the next day, Vickie was the last one in the locker room, packing up her bag. She threw it in her locker and clasped the padlock around the latch. Before she walked out, she stepped in front of a mirror that hung on the wall.

With a smile, she puffed her chest out. *Look at you, fitting in. You're making friends, you're surviving, and best of all, nobody knows you're a vampire. Keep your instincts under control, and you'll do fine. You're becoming a normal teenager.*

That last thought gave her pause. "A normal teenager?" What did that really mean? Was she not "normal" before? For a moment, she wondered if she was leaving her vampire heritage behind.

Of course, that was the point. She shook the thought off and headed for the door, ready to go home.

She turned the corner and stepped out of the locker room to see, to her surprise, Eric standing in the hall waiting for her.

Vickie tried her best not to blush. *What is it about him, anyway? Why do I get so excited to see him?*

It took a little effort, but she managed to play it cool. "What's up?"

"Hey." He smiled at her. "I was talking to Coach. It sounds like you're really fitting in nicely on the team."

Vickie pumped her fist—she'd seen the quarterback do that during the Packer game and thought it was a fun way to display excitement. She tried it, and it felt good. "That's great. I had a feeling. Everyone is so nice to me so far."

"Yeah, the girls are always nicer than the guys."

They fell into step beside one another. "Did you have to go through initiation when you joined the team?"

He hung his head and grabbed the straps on his backpack. "Oh, definitely. I had bubbler rides, like, every day for a week. And they gave me an atomic wedgie." She looked at him, her gaze focused, puzzled by the comment. "Okay, so that's when they pick you up by your underwear and lift you off the ground."

"Ouch."

"Darn right, ouch. They got the waistband over my head. The seniors tried to rip the waistband so they could hang it up in the locker room as a trophy. They did that with all the freshmen that year. But because I wore new underwear, it wouldn't rip. It simply stretched and stretched. Man, it hurt. Then I had to hobble home with my underwear waistband up by my armpits." Vickie stifled a laugh. "It's fine, I'm over it. Go ahead and laugh."

"Boy, the guys and the girls sure are different."

"That's what I hear. So depending on how you race on

Friday, do you think you'll go to Minnesota at the end of the month?"

She ran her fingers through her hair, a little distracted. "Oh…I'm not sure. I didn't know about Minnesota. What's that?"

"There's a big national race the team goes to every year in Minnesota. The race itself isn't that big a deal, but it's a fun trip for those who go. It's only for Varsity runners and is so much fun. It's an overnight excursion, so you have a long road trip with your friends, then you all stay in a hotel for a night. There's a pool and a hot tub. It's great team bonding."

Vickie's thoughts slid from one extreme to the other as she considered it. *Oh man, that does sound like fun. But can I trust myself to be away from my new family already? What if I screw something up? What if I wake in the middle of the night with my fangs bared or something? That might not be a great idea.*

"Well, I only ask because it's the last weekend of this month." Eric inhaled through his clenched teeth. "So, you know…"

"No, I don't." He pointed to a poster on the wall for Homecoming Weekend—which was being held on the same weekend. "Oh, so Homecoming is that weekend, too? What is that?"

"Wow." Eric tried not to sound insulting, but he was surprised to see how little she knew. "Homecoming Weekend is huge. There's a pep rally on Friday, then the big football game on Saturday. Saturday night is the Homecoming Dance."

"Oh, like a ball?"

He chuckled. "Kinda. You do dress up fancy and you go out with your friends. Usually, we get a group together for dinner and then go to the dance."

"That sounds like fun, too."

"It is. This year, though, I have a chance to go to Minnesota because I'm on the Varsity team. I've wanted to go on this trip for a while so I'm annoyed that it's scheduled at the same time as Homecoming."

"Wow, that's a real bummer," Vickie said and meant it, but she was also really proud of herself for using the word "bummer" in a sentence. She'd overheard it in her algebra class and decided to use it. "So which do you want? Would you rather go on the trip or would you rather go to Homecoming?"

He paused for a second as they continued down the hall. The school was so empty, they felt like they were the only ones in the entire building. The silence hung in the air like a heavy blanket.

"I'd rather go to Homecoming if I had a date. I expect, since you didn't even know what Homecoming was, you don't have a date yourself yet, do you?"

"No, I don't. I didn't know you were even supposed to have one."

Another even longer silence stretched awkwardly between them.

Eric grew so nervous and self-conscious that sweat started to soak the clean shirt he'd thrown on after practice. His palms were clammy and shaking, but as they approached the doors leading to the parking lot, he couldn't bring himself to say anything else.

Vickie was confused. *Why isn't he saying anything? Is he*

waiting for me to say something? Is he trying to communicate something by being silent? What's going on? Is this normal?

A set of headlights shone in the dark. "That's…my uncle." She felt weird calling Craig that. She had never referred to him as uncle out loud.

They walked to the SUV. Craig rolled down the windows to greet them both. "Hey, guys."

"Hey…Uncle Craig."

"Hi, Mr. Watson."

Uncle Craig? Really? Craig tried not to react to it because he knew he had to play it off as normal. He waved to Eric, who said goodbye to Vickie and continued across the parking lot as she climbed in.

"Uncle Craig?" he asked.

"I can't call you Dad out there. I'm Alexis' cousin at school."

"Oh. Good thinking." This situation still confused everyone. "So…you and Eric seem to be getting close."

"Oh, he's a great friend."

"Do you think you guys would date? You said he's cute."

"No. I don't know. I'm not sure how any of this works yet." She shifted in her seat and looked out the window, hoping to avoid any more awkward conversation.

Do I tell her the story about Katie? Maybe she would learn a thing or two from that. Nah…I'll wait for her to ask for help. She probably wouldn't listen right now anyway.

———

Later that night, Alexis and Vickie were getting ready for bed, brushing their hair and washing their faces.

"Hey, so Homecoming is coming up." Vickie tapped Alexis on the shoulder.

"Yeah, so?"

"How does that work?"

Alexis laughed. "How does what work?"

"There's a dance, right? How do you get a date for the dance?"

The other girl ran the brush through her hair. "Do you want a date? I've never had a date for Homecoming. I always went with a group of friends. Last year, it was me, Jess, Jamie, and Eric. We went out to a nice dinner and then to the dance and partied the night away. It was fun."

Vickie looked somewhat disappointed as she finished filing one of her toenails.

Alexis tilted her head. "Who do you want to go with? Eric?" Vickie nodded. "Did he ask you?"

"No. I thought he would, but then he didn't. He kept talking about Homecoming. I didn't even know you had dates for that sort of thing."

"Mm-hmm. Well, I would wait. If he's thinking about asking you, he probably will soon. So give him a little more time to muster up the courage. Sometimes, boys can be nervous about that sort of thing."

"Are you sure?"

"Yeah. And look, if you want to go with him but he doesn't ask you, I'm sure we'll all go together either way. So you can be with him even if he's not your official date. It'll be fun."

Vickie stood and walked out into the hallway. "Yeah, if he goes."

"Why wouldn't he go?"

"He said he'll go to Minnesota for a cross country race if he doesn't have a date."

Alexis raised her eyebrows in surprise. "He told you that directly? Then we have a little dance to do ourselves. Give him a few more days. If he's talked to you about it, then he wants to go with you. If he doesn't ask you by… like, the end of next week, then ask him yourself."

"Is that proper?" Vickie thought of the arranged marriages of her day and balked at the prospect. The girl never had a say in anything like that. The thought of having to ask a boy to a dance in any kind of romantic fashion made her squeamish.

"Don't worry about proper. It's the twenty-first century. All you need to worry about is to make sure he's at that dance, whether that's with us in a group or with you as a date."

They both said goodnight and went their separate ways. As Alexis stepped into her bedroom and closed the door, she leaned up against it.

I'm happy for her. I don't like Eric like that so it doesn't bother me for that reason. So why does is it bother me at all? I want them to be together and I want them to be happy.

But what if they get together and it doesn't work out? Eric is one of my best friends. And Vickie is basically my sister now. If they have a bad breakup, I'll be stuck in the middle of it. I can't have that.

She moved over to her little Christmas tree and flipped the switch to illuminate the fiber-optic lights and fill the room with a multi-colored glow.

You're overthinking this. As long as you are friends with both of them, you will help them. Your time will come. Listen to your dad. Be supportive.

Alexis laid down on her bed, rested her head on her pillow, and stared at the colors that danced on the ceiling.

Your time will come.

CHAPTER TWENTY

As she closed her bedroom door, Vickie felt overwhelmed by a sense of community.

In short order, she had joined a high school, made a few friends, joined the cross country team, made a few more friends, established a positive identity for herself, and now was even talking about going to a school dance with a boy.

She stared into the mirror on the back of her door and smiled. *You don't only look human right now, Vickie. You feel human. You are human. You are a normal teenage girl going to school, playing sports, and thinking about boys.*

A big, tooth-filled smile brightened her face. But as she stared at her herself in the mirror, she was reminded once again about her heritage.

Her fangs, while they didn't stick out, were a little pointier than the other teeth in her mouth. It wasn't noticeable to anyone but her—at least, that's what she thought.

She moved closer to the mirror so her face was only a few inches from it, and she craned her neck to get a better look at her teeth. Her forehead scrunched in a frown, she ran her tongue along them.

You may feel like a human, Vickie. But never forget that you are a vampire. You are the last vampire, and that means you need to embrace and celebrate your heritage in any way you can.

Vickie felt guilt weigh heavily on her shoulders as if this focus on being a normal human being had pulled her away from who she really was.

She sat on the floor, crossed her legs, and slid her laptop into her lap. A few days earlier, she had found a website called Reddit. It was full of smaller communities of people linked around different interests and groups.

One group was focused primarily around real-life vampires. She didn't have time to look at it when she found it, so she had bookmarked it for later.

Now that she had a little time, she opened the website and started reading. The few posts she read made her feel a little weird.

This is really a group for people who are into vampires or dating vampires. That's kinda gross. Though it's nice to know there are people who aren't turned off by vampires, anyway.

Still, they weren't exactly into the type of vampire Vickie was. They seemed to be preoccupied with biters. Every post had something to do with drinking blood or sucking blood, which she honestly found repulsive.

It was the closest she had come to anybody interested in real-life vampires, so on a whim, she clicked on the **Create An Account** link in the top corner of the page.

A name? Okay, Vickie. Taken. How about VickieVampire? Perfect. Nobody can see who I am, anyway. Why not? Maybe online, I can still be a vampire, even if I have to keep it quiet in real life.

Once the account was created, she started a new post in the vampires' group:

Hi everyone.

My name is Vickie. I'm a vampire who recently moved to Milwaukee. I'm only a teenager, but I wanted to connect with people who aren't afraid of me for being one. I am only looking to preserve a strong connection to my vampire roots. But I'm a non-biter, just so you know. I wondered if there are any others out there. I doubt it because I think I'm the last one. Still, I thought I'd take a chance. I'd love to hear from you.

Vickie

Within minutes, the little mail icon in the corner of her screen lit with messages. It seemed like there were new replies and comments from people every minute.

Wow. Maybe there are other vampires out there. Or, at least, vampire supporters. Is there a place I can go to be myself again?

She clicked on the icon and scanned through the messages. Immediately, she felt sickened. Most of the messages were from strange people who seemed obsessed with the typical false vampire stuff like drinking blood. Some of them offered to meet her, but she was not interested.

Ugh. Maybe this was a mistake.

She closed her laptop and looked in the mirror again. *Who is this girl? Who are you? The girl in the mirror here isn't a vampire. She's not Vickie Brommer. She's Vickie Hewitt, the cross country runner at Clear Lake High School.*

She ripped her clothes off, opened the closet door, and pulled out the yellowed white gown she had spent four hundred years in. After pulling it on over her head and sticking her arms through the sleeves, she looked in the mirror again.

That's the girl. That's Vickie Brommer. You're still in there.

On top of her dresser sat the old chalice with her family's crest carved into the side. She held it every day as a reminder of her old family. Tears welled up in her eyes as she grabbed it and clutched it close to her, running her fingers along the sides once again. *I'm sorry. I'm not turning my back on you, I promise. This is so much harder than I thought it would be for me. I want to keep going, but how do I do that and still be a vampire?*

The walls of her room felt like they were closing in on her. She looked at the clock. *It's after 11:00 pm. Everybody is probably asleep by now.*

Slowly and silently, she turned her doorknob and opened the bedroom door. The house was dark and quiet. She stepped out into the hallway. *I only need some fresh air.* As quietly as possible, she eased the lock on the back door and opened it. A cold blast of air rushed in and made her shiver.

She didn't care. In fact, a part of her welcomed it. Vickie walked outside where the cold of the night could wrap around her body for a moment.

The house was not located in the nicest of neighborhoods. If she walked around the streets—especially dressed in that gown—she would draw too much attention from the wrong kind of crowd.

Regardless, she didn't want to walk. She wanted to do something else.

Vickie was out there to be a vampire.

She walked barefoot across the back yard, circled the pool, and allowed her emotions to bubble up inside her. Secure in the knowledge that she was alone, she bared her teeth and sighed as her fangs protruded slowly from her mouth.

The feeling made her smile. She had so much pent-up vampire energy inside her that it was a relief to let some of it out.

Behind the house was a large field which had been dug out into an overflow reservoir for neighborhood flooding. On the far side of the reservoir was a small group of trees —not quite a forest, but more than a few.

Vickie stood at the hill at the far end of the yard, crouched down, and leaned forward. *I am still a vampire.*

In a flash, she raced away at full speed. The grass and dirt almost tore open beneath her feet as she ran. In the blink of an eye, she was on the other side of the reservoir and smiled from ear to ear.

She repeated the sprint a few times and pumped her legs as fast as she could. It was a short trip for such speed, but it was enough for her to feel like a vampire once again.

Finally, she stopped the exercise and remained near the trees. she could feel her super-strength course through her limbs like a massive adrenaline rush. Vaulting into an upward leap, she caught hold of a high branch and climbed to the top of one of the trees.

The wind blew the branches hard and she raised her arms into the air. Her gown billowed and her hair caught the wind like a kite hovering in the sky. She threw her head back and looked at the glowing face of the moon, which was the only light shining that high above the earth.

Vickie drew a long, deep breath through her nose and laughed with real relief. *I feel so free. For the first time in four hundred years, I feel free.*

She dropped to the ground again, still itching to use that super-strength. A felled tree lay in the dirt, so she wrapped her arms around it, lifted it over her head, and tossed it up with ease.

It crashed into the ground with a thud that shook the area like an earthquake. She even stumbled a little with the force of it. As she walked around in freedom, she heard car tires squeal and grow louder. *I've made too much noise. Someone is onto me. I'd better go.*

With a smile, she unleashed her super-speed again. To get it out of her system, she ran to the house and back a few times. *Nobody will tell me to slow down here. It feels so good to run at full speed again and not have to fit into some group.*

The freedom was intoxicating, but once she reached the back yard of the house again, she saw headlights shining in the trees. Someone stepped out of their truck and now yelled at the top of his lungs about what they'd witnessed.

Vickie laughed quietly. *You have to be a little more careful than that, I guess.*

But the little adventure had served its purpose. For a few minutes, she had felt like a vampire again. She shook her head at the commotion in the distance as she returned to her room once she'd locked the back door behind her.

Carefully, she hung the gown in the closet again, a little dirtier than when she'd put it on. She slipped her pajamas on and looked in the mirror again with a regretful sigh. *Back to being human again. It was fun while it lasted, though.*

The next morning, over breakfast, Craig greeted the two girls at the table. "Did either of you hear that loud crash late last night? It sounded like a car crash or something. I almost leapt out of bed to see what it was."

Vickie smiled inwardly, although she took care to keep her expression neutral. *Thank goodness he didn't come out to investigate. I would've been in trouble, for sure.*

"I was out cold last night," Alexis said. "I had a long day. I don't think an earthquake could've woken me up."

"Oh, yeah, me either," Vickie said. She lowered her gaze and shoved another spoonful of cereal into her mouth.

CHAPTER TWENTY-ONE

Living in the twenty-first century often felt like a dream to Vickie.

During her childhood, she rarely spent time in any locations outside of her home or the village. An entire world existed beyond her immediate life—a world she never interacted with.

Since she awoke, she had been on airplanes and driven in cars. She now lived in a completely new part of the planet, and she'd traveled for miles within that area as well.

And that didn't include the mind-blowing amount of information she could process simply by sitting at her laptop.

But for all the technology available to her in the twenty-first century and all the different places that she could go, one of her favorite places to spend time in was the school library.

Books were her connection to the past. She understood them. Her castle had a library with a handful of them, and she loved being able to leaf through the pages and read what somebody else had written and documented.

When she sat at one of the study tables in the Clear Lake High School library, however, she stared at the stacks and stacks of books in awe at how many there were. She didn't even have to open any of them.

"I still don't understand why this place gives you such a rush." Alexis kept her voice to a whisper to avoid having their library privileges revoked.

Vickie dragged her gaze away from the books to face her friend. "I know there's more information on the Internet. My laptop gives me access to nearly everything in the known world. But I can't feel that. It's there, but it's not like I can click a button and sense how vast the Internet is. Here? I can see how many books there are. They're everywhere, and I can compare this to the few books I had growing up. It's an emotional thing for me, I guess."

This explanation amused Alexis. *Sometimes, having someone around who didn't grow up like you did offers you a little different perspective on the world. I suppose this is good for me.*

The girls sat at a round table near the center of the library itself. Clear Lake High School had a relatively small library—one floor, with dozens of shelves surrounding the tables. On the far wall stood a computer lab with rows of desks for students to bring their own laptops, along with a handful of desktop computers waiting for those who didn't have their own devices.

Both girls had Study Hall, although they were in different classrooms. At Clear Lake, a student could spend their Study Hall period in a few different places. The previous year, Alexis would go to the Music Hall and sign in. It was a haven where she could relax, play the piano, or simply enjoy studying while not seated at an actual desk for a change.

Since Vickie was not in the music program, she couldn't sign into the Music Hall. Instead, she enjoyed spending her time in the library, and Alexis joined her there. The two of them liked the ability to catch up and check on each other in the middle of the school routine.

On an average day, they would chat a little, then return to studying. But on that particular afternoon, Vickie was preoccupied. "What's the story between Eric and Jess?"

"Story?" Alexis looked up from her homework. "What do you mean?"

"Is there a history between them? They seem to flirt with each other often. Did they date? Or are they dating now? What is it?"

The other girl snorted so hard that one of the librarians looked up from the front desk with a frown. She stifled her laughter and nodded to the old woman as if to say, "I know, I'm sorry. I'll try to be quieter."

She shook off the laughing fit. "Jess and Eric are the furthest thing from dating. Trust me. If you really have your sights set on Eric, Jess is the least of your worries."

"Then why do they act like that?"

"They're like brother and sister. They're really good friends, but they aren't dating. Neither of them has ever admitted to having feelings for the other. And I'm close with both of them. Trust me, they're fine." Vickie returned her gaze to the bookshelves on the other side of the room while Alexis watched her face. "Why are you talking to me about this, anyway? Talk to Eric. If you like him, ask him."

"I don't want to. It's inappropriate."

She closed her textbook and rested her elbows on it. "At some point, you'll have to let go of this inappropriate stuff. You live in a different world now. Girls can take the initiative whenever they want to. If I'm telling you to talk to him, you can be sure you're safe."

The vampire didn't respond.

"It has nothing to do with inappropriate, does it?" Alexis lowered her head. "You're scared."

Vickie puffed her chest out. "No, I'm not. What would I be scared of?"

"Of boys. Come on. You're scared of asking a boy out. We both know he wants to go to Homecoming with you. So walk up to him and be like, 'Hey, Eric, want to go to Homecoming with me?' He'll say, yes, and the two of you can live happily ever after together."

"I don't even know if I want to go with him to the dance."

"Oh, please. Yes, you do." Alexis shook her head with a smile. "Quit lying."

"No, it's not that. I do want to go with him. But he also wants to go to Minnesota with the team. Maybe if I don't ask him, he can go and have fun with them instead."

Her friend leaned back with a skeptical look on her face. "I know Eric. If he has to choose between going to a dance with a cute girl and going to a cross country meet, he'll choose the cute girl every time. Ask him. Do it the next time you see him."

Vickie grew annoyed at her badgering. "Hey, what about you?"

"Me?"

"You haven't asked anyone. You're walking around, telling me to get over myself and ask a boy out when you don't even bother to do that yourself. Take your own advice."

"Excuse me, but I don't really know any boy who interests me right now. And definitely none that make me want to go to a dance. I don't have a date because I don't want a date." *What a liar you are. You'd go to Homecoming with the school janitor if he asked you. Why don't you admit that you don't think anyone would go with you?* "Besides, we usually go to these things in a group—all of us friends. It's more fun that way." *It's not more fun, it's less risk. You simply don't want to take a chance on wasting your night with a guy you don't like.*

"We can still go in a group." Vickie shrugged her shoulders in confusion. "Why wouldn't we still go together?"

"Because if you go with a date, you'll want to have a nice little dinner on your own and some time to get to know each other. At the end of the night, you walk to the door and maybe kiss...all that romantic stuff. You can't do that if you go in a group. Everybody would be watching you."

Vickie's eyes widened. "You think I would go with Eric alone?" The librarian shushed them again from the front desk. Vickie lowered her voice. "This is my first high school dance. I don't want to go without you."

"Seriously?" *The way she's been getting the hang of things, I assumed she wanted some independence.*

"Alexis, this is a brand-new social situation for me. I

don't know how to act. I don't know how to dance. I need my best friend there to nudge me if I'm embarrassing myself. And if this winds up being some kind of date with Eric? Then I definitely need you there."

Alexis gave her a sympathetic smile. *Sometimes, I forget how new everything is to her. It's not like I'm some dating expert, but still...* "Okay. If you guys go together, we can still make sure that we all go as a group. It'll take the pressure off you."

Vickie sighed with relief. "I'm still not asking him. I can't wrap my head around that. But then we have to get a date for you."

"Oh, no we don't." Alexis raised her palms in protest. "I can still simply go on my own." *What are you worried about? Aren't there guys you'd go with? Would it really be that bad to have a date for a change?*

"If Eric and I are on a date, we all need to partner up. That would make it feel a little more natural, wouldn't it?"

I suddenly wish we were back to doing homework. "We don't want to put any more pressure on this than there already will be. We can go as the regular group—you, me, Eric, Jess, and Jamie. You and Eric can be on a date, but we'll treat it like a regular hang. Trust me, you both will be more comfortable. Otherwise, it'll feel like too much and maybe one of you will freak out."

"Freak out?" Vickie squinted at her. "What is that supposed to mean?"

"Like, if you put a lot of pressure on it to work right away, you could sabotage the whole thing."

"So you're saying it might not work?"

Don't freak her out, Alexis. Choose your words carefully.

"Sometimes, it works. Sometimes, it doesn't. Did you think you would marry Eric right away?"

"I'm fourteen years old. These are prime marrying years."

"Whoa, whoa, whoa." Alexis fought the urge to raise her voice, not wanting to get kicked out of the library. "Look around you, Vickie. Do you see anyone else married? Or even thinking about being married? Am I married? These are dating years, not marriage years." *Yeah, right. They're dating years for everyone except you.*

Vickie folded her hands in front of her. *You are forgetting that you live in a different time. Culture today is different than before. Teenagers don't marry. You keep forgetting that. When you went into that box, you were starting to feel anxious for a suitor. Nowadays, there are suitors everywhere. Don't pin all your hopes on Eric. You'll scare him away.*

Alexis noticed the vampire getting lost in her thoughts. "You probably won't marry Eric. But that doesn't mean you can't date him. I only want you to be aware of the fact that you might break up. That will make things really awkward for me."

"I don't want to hurt you or cause you any problems. Maybe I won't date him. I'll wait around and find somebody else."

"No, you won't."

"Yes, I will. If I put your friendship with Eric at risk, then I will wait until another suitor comes along."

Alexis smirked at the word suitor. *She's such an old-fashioned girl. Don't be a jerk to her. She's not trying to cause any problems between you and Eric and doesn't want to take over your life. Right now, she's only finding her footing. Be support-*

ive. "We'll cross that bridge when we get there. Don't worry about that part. Go with Eric to the dance and we'll work out the rest of it."

"That's assuming he asks me."

She reached out and grabbed Vickie's arm. "Trust me. He will ask you. I know the look he gets in his eyes when he likes a girl. He has that look with you." The vampire smiled when she heard that. "He'll find the courage to ask you eventually. But if you wait around too long, ask him. It'll be fine."

Vickie nodded, but she still disagreed with the notion. *If he doesn't ask me, I need a backup plan. I don't want to lose him to Minnesota. He said if he didn't have a date to the dance, he would go on the Minnesota trip.*

I'll have to make sure I'm on that trip. Then, no matter what he decides to do, I can spend that weekend with him.

CHAPTER TWENTY-TWO

A stiff breeze swirled a pile of dry, brown leaves across the grass at McCarty Park when the bus squealed to a halt at the sidewalk.

It was the Friday of the first cross country meet of the season. On the bus ride over, Vickie squirmed in her uniform and Krista giggled at her. "It takes some getting used to. I think they're comfortable."

The vampire, however, came from a much more conservative time. Under her swishy pants and windbreaker was a pair of very short blue running shorts and a red, white, and blue tank top sporting the school colors and Viking mascot. The thought of taking her coat and pants off to run in that outfit swelled a pit of nerves in her stomach that she couldn't shake.

"Are you nervous?" Krista asked her.

"A little. I haven't raced before."

"It's okay. Just go out there, run hard, pace yourself, and have fun. It's your first race. You don't need to win it or anything."

That was where Krista was wrong—at least, Vickie thought she might be wrong. *I don't want to win the race because I don't want to stand out too much. But if I win the race, I could get put on the Varsity team.*

It was all part of her master plan to address her concerns over Homecoming Weekend. She was running the Junior Varsity race that afternoon. JV runners did not have the option to go on the Minnesota road trip. That privilege was reserved for Varsity runners.

Be a Varsity runner, and you can go wherever Eric wants to go.

Coach Lueck stood at the front of the bus after it stopped to address the team. "Okay, everybody. Here we go—the first meet of the season. We want to start strong this year, so everybody run hard, use your teammates, and use the other runners. I want to come home with some medals today so we can build confidence. I have my eye on that championship trophy this year." The team cheered. He looked at a piece of paper folded in half. "The first race is the JV boys, then the JV girls, followed by the Varsity boys and the Varsity girls. When we get off the bus, I want to see everyone set up camp right away where I have us marked off. JV teams, start warming up right away. Let's go."

The bus doors swung open and the runners poured out. Directly in front of them was a section of picnic tables surrounded by a string of flags and a banner that read *Clear Lake Vikings.*

Vickie followed Krista. They ducked under the flags and dropped their bags off.

The coach clambered onto a picnic table and pointed to

a hill in the distance. "The starting line is over there. Teams, I want you to warm up by walk-running the course. Get a feel for the terrain and know where you're going. JV runners, saddle up."

"Over here, girls." One of Vickie's teammates—a senior named Laura—waved her arm to motion them toward her, and all the younger runners, including Vickie, gathered as a group.

Together, they jogged to the starting line, then followed the arrows to jog the course. After about half a mile, they stopped to walk for a while.

The concept of a warmup amused Vickie. Her powers allowed her to run as fast as she wanted instantaneously. But if the team warmed up, she had to pretend to as well.

Besides, even if her legs didn't need it, she wanted to know where the course went. She could follow the pack, but she had a more aggressive goal for the day.

In her mind, the only way to guarantee that she would be a Varsity runner would be to win the race. The night before, she'd sat Alexis down and told her what she wanted to do.

"You know that'll make you stand out, right?" Her friend had literally winced. "I'm not saying that's a bad thing. I'm saying we have to be careful. You're setting expectations here."

Vickie had made her mind up, however. "I know. But that's okay. Right now, standing out isn't a big concern for me. I want to be on that Varsity team by the end of the month. So how do I win this race without raising any red flags?"

Alexis sat on her bed and retrieved her laptop. "Well, I would say you want to win the race but not set a world record or anything." She pulled up race results from the previous year's JV girls. "It looks like the winners of these races all run around seventeen minutes for a five-K race. Let me punch that into a calculator here...and that's a 5:30 mile." Alexis smiled with satisfaction.

"Is that good?"

"When you tried out for the team with Coach Lueck on the track, you ran a 5:30 mile. So this is perfect. You can run that and be consistent with what you've already done. Keep that pace, then beat whoever's at the front of the race once you can see the finish line."

It sounds simple enough.

After they ran-walked the course, the team moved to the starting line to cheer on the JV boys.

A volunteer shouted into a megaphone and held a starter's pistol in the air. "On your mark...get set..."

Bang.

Vickie wasn't prepared for the sound of a gun firing. Her head snapped to the right and she looked anxiously in the direction of the shooter. She gritted her teeth, and her fangs pushed down and out.

Fortunately for her, the rest of the team around her paid attention to the runners who launched from the starting line to clap and cheer them on with words of encouragement. She came to her senses and clamped her lips together until her heart rate steadied and the fangs retracted.

Coach Lueck jogged past the JV girls team. "Girls, go

stretch and continue to warm up. You can cheer the other teams after your race, okay? Get your heads ready for this race." He continued to another part of the course to announce splits for the boys.

The girls walked back to the picnic tables and began stretching. A few pulled off their windbreakers to sit in tank tops and pants, although it was still a little chilly for that.

"Are you ready to go?"

Vickie grinned at Craig and Alexis, who both wore large smiles. "Your first big race. Our little athlete," Alexis teased. "Seriously, though, how are you feeling?"

"A little nervous, I guess." Vickie bent her knee and leaned down to stretch her hamstring since the girl next to her did the same thing. "I hope I do well." *And by well, I mean win without making anyone suspicious that I'm a supernatural being with the power to run faster than any human alive.*

Alexis winked at her. "You'll do fine. Go out there and have some fun. And remember to hit those splits we talked about. Do you have your watch on?"

Vickie held her wrist up to showcase the new runner's watch Craig bought her earlier in the week.

"It looks good," he said. "You'll kill it out there."

"We'll leave you to get your head in the race," Alexis said. "But we'll see you out there on the course. Come on, Dad, I want a hot dog." They both walked away in the direction of the concession stands.

About half an hour later, Vickie stood anxiously at the starting line with the other JV girls. The shorts were so revealing, she felt like she might as well have been naked. A quick survey of the other girls at the starting line showed that basically every team wore similar running shorts. The boys did, too, which at least soothed some of her nerves.

Still, she kept her hands instinctively at her sides and held her thighs as if that could cover them somehow.

This time, she was prepared for the starter's pistol. She and the other girls started the race and everyone activated the timers on their watches as they put one foot in front of the other and settled into a steady pace.

Right at the start of the race, Vickie was not prepared to feel so anxious. With more than a hundred runners all coming off the same starting line to run the course, there was a tough bottleneck to negotiate.

The vampire alternated between watching what was happening in front of her and looking down to make sure she didn't accidentally kick anyone or trip a runner.

Soon, she found herself in the middle of the pack while the course narrowed. She couldn't pass anyone, to her frustration, and she had to wait until later in the race when the course opened up a little more.

At the completion of the first mile, she looked at her watch. *Seven minutes? Come on, Vickie, you can't get on the Varsity team running that slowly. Let's go.*

Earlier that week, Coach Lueck had joined the JV girls on a run and talked racing strategy with them. His words echoed in Vickie's head as she pushed forward.

"The key to racing is to beat one runner at a time," he said. "Pick a pack of runners, catch up to them, settle in, then look ahead to the next pack of runners. Burst forward, catch up to them, settle in, and keep repeating.

That's how you fight through a race. It's not only about running fast. It's about running smart."

It was the perfect strategy for Vickie because she could move ahead in the race without looking too suspicious.

One by one, she chose her runners and darted ahead with only a little extra kick—enough to cover ground, but not so much that she turned heads.

Other runners, however, couldn't believe the speed at which she moved. More than one ran with their mouths hanging open while she disappeared in the distance.

At the two-mile marker, Alexis and her father waited.

"Do you think she can keep it under control?" he asked under his breath, his expression a little tense.

"We talked about it. She knows what times she has to maintain. But there are many runners ahead of her. She'll have to be careful not to run too quickly, but she has to make up a lot still if she wants to win."

By the time Alexis finished that sentence, Vickie materialized from over the hill. She crossed the two-mile marker and nodded at her family with confidence before she glanced at her watch.

12:03. That means I ran that mile in four minutes. Only a little farther now and I can settle down.

"She's a little slow." Alexis shook her head as she checked the time on her watch. "I hope she knows what she's doing." But she didn't know that Vickie had picked up her speed considerably.

A little farther ahead on the course, Coach Lueck greeted her with applause. "All right, Vickie. Strong race. You're the lead runner on the team." He jogged alongside her as he shouted. "If you feel comfortable, go get the lead runner and win this thing." He stopped jogging and she continued, and although he shouted after her, his words seemed to simply echo in the distance behind her. "You're in the home stretch. If you have afterburners, turn 'em on and go."

Vickie smirked. *If he only knew what my afterburners looked like.*

She stared at the lead runner—a redhead with a ponytail that swayed like a bronzed pendulum. The girl was as thin as a rail and an experienced runner in her own right.

Confidently, Vickie sidled up beside her and listened to her heave and suck air. They turned the corner and the vampire saw the finish line. *Time to turn it on.*

With one more glance at her opponent, she pumped her legs a little faster, barreled downhill to the finish line, and crossed it to win the race by a margin of about ten seconds. She hit the STOP button on her watch.

16:42.

She pumped her fist. *That's a Varsity time*

The crowd of Clear Lake supporters clapped and cheered and patted her on the back while she moved through the chute. Volunteers tore off the bottom portion of the number attached to the front of her shirt, and she walked out of the chute to her coach, who raised his hand for a high-five with a huge smile on his face.

"Not bad for your first race, huh?" He nearly bounced with excitement at the potential of this raw runner in front of him. "Do you think you can do that again next week?"

"Sure," Vickie replied.

"I think you earned yourself a spot on the Varsity team. Way to go."

That news excited her. So did the medal she was awarded at the ceremony after all the races were over.

But even more exciting to her was the hug Eric gave her when he congratulated her before they got on the bus.

That was why she won the race to begin with.

CHAPTER TWENTY-THREE

The next Monday, Vickie was flying high.

She leapt out of bed at 5:00 am and practically sang in the shower. Things were great. She had lined up her chances to spend Homecoming Weekend with Eric, she was the new hero of the cross country team, her coach was proud of her, and she was making friends.

For all her struggles with letting go of her vampire roots, her new life as a human couldn't have started off any better. She even felt so good, she wanted to try to make breakfast.

In all honesty, she hadn't paid very close attention to the other members of the family when they made breakfast. But she knew the basics and how to work the appliances. *How hard could it be?*

Since everyone else still dragged their way out of bed, Vickie wanted to be nice and surprise them with eggs and toast.

She pulled the carton of eggs and the loaf of bread out

onto the counter beside the toaster. Then, she placed a frying pan on the stove and turned the burner on. *I want it hot so it cooks the eggs all the way through. I'll put it to high. If that's too hot, I'll simply stir it and it'll cook faster.*

With a confident spring in her step, she slid four slices of bread into the toaster. Using the same logic, she turned the toaster up to ten.

Once the pan was hot, she assumed one egg per person would be enough. *I can always make more.* Vickie cracked the eggs and dropped them one at a time onto the pan, which sizzled and crackled as the food made contact with the nonstick surface.

Very quickly, smoke poured from the pan. *Stir, stir, stir!* But because she had failed to spray any oil onto the pan, the egg adhered to the surface and quickly turned black in the overheated pan. The smoke continued to billow up, and she scraped with a spatula to try to loosen the ruined mess, to no avail.

To her surprise, even more smoke now issued from the toaster, which had almost instantly transformed the slices of bread into charcoal. She abandoned the hot pan to press the cancel button on the appliance.

She scowled at the blackened remains of the bread and scratched her head in confusion. *If it does that, why make a toaster go up that high? Who wants ruined bread?*

As she mulled that over, she forgot about the smoke still issuing from the burnt eggs, which were completely ruined and well and truly cemented to the pan. The entire kitchen was now full of so much smoke that it was hard to see. She squinted through the haze and startled when the smoke detector blared an alarm.

The loud beeping sent her into a flurry, her fangs bared. She squeezed the handle of the pan so hard, it shattered and pieces of plastic erupted to scatter at her feet.

Craig sprinted out of his room in a t-shirt and pajama pants, shouting, "What is going on out here?" He ran to the smoke detector at the top of the basement stairs, unhooked it, and removed the battery. His ears were still ringing as he surveyed the damage.

"I… I only wanted to make breakfast." Vickie stared at him with a spooked expression on her face, utterly embarrassed at the carnage she'd caused.

He shook his head, amused, while he pulled the patio door open to release the smoke. "That's very nice of you. Maybe wait until we can show you how to make breakfast. Since I'm wide awake now, how about I go pick up breakfast for everyone? I can't use that pan anymore anyway."

"I'm sorry about that. I'll clean it up."

"The broom is next to the fridge." He grabbed his keys and walked out the side door to his SUV.

Vickie swept up the remnants of plastic on the floor while Alexis stumbled out of her room in her pajamas. "What the heck is going on?"

"I wanted to make breakfast for everybody." The vampire sighed. "I was in a good mood."

"And now you're not? That's okay. It was an accident. It's still really nice of you." She walked past her to grab a drink of water from the faucet.

"No, that's not what I mean."

Vickie dumped the last of the shattered pan into the garbage, then paused and stared at the floor.

"Are you okay?" Alexis returned the glass to the counter beside the sink. "You look like you're not feeling well."

"I'm not…but I don't know why."

"Is it your head? Your stomach? What's going on?"

She placed her hand on her stomach. "It's my gut, but it's not like sickness. It's just… I suddenly have a bad feeling about today."

"What do you mean?" Her sister walked over to the kitchen table, pulled out a chair, and sat. She folded her arms to shield herself from the breeze that blew in through the patio door.

"It simply feels weird. I don't know what it is. A sense that something's wrong." She returned the broom to its place next to the fridge.

"Is that a vampire thing?"

"It can be. But that's usually if you run into other vampires or other supernatural beings. It can't be that." *Can it? I'm the last one. And there weren't any on this side of the world to begin with. I wouldn't have this sense if another vampire back in Austria woke up, would I? I'm way too far away.*

"Well, I'm not a werewolf or anything, so you're safe."

After they ate breakfast and Alexis showered, the girls went off to school. As they stepped through the door into the building, Vickie stopped again and shook her head.

"It's worse now. I have a really bad feeling."

"Are you sure it's not the flu or something?" Alexis put her hand on her shoulder. "Maybe you need to go home and lie down."

"No, it's not that. Trust me. This is bad but I don't know why."

They sat with their friends in their customary place during the early morning hour. Eric slept as usual, but the girls chatted easily. Vickie didn't join in the conversation. She couldn't, too distracted by the weird feeling in the pit of her stomach.

The bell for the first period rang, and her stomach tightened further. *What is going on? Why do I feel like this? Is this how my dad felt when he whisked me away to the box? Some sense of impending doom?*

With every step she took, she felt a stronger sense of danger. By the time she reached the algebra class, the fire burned furiously in her gut.

The next bell rang, and everyone took their seats at their desks. Vickie turned to look around the room, but no one did anything that could possibly have caused her alarm. *It has to be my imagination. Maybe it's something I ate. Or the smoke. Yeah, that could be it. I inhaled a lot of smoke. My vampire system has probably gone haywire from that.*

She did her best to shake it off and pay attention in class. For a while, she managed reasonably well—until there was a knock at the door.

Her gaze immediately darted to the entrance, and her fangs poked her lips. She kept her mouth shut while a stunningly handsome boy stepped into the room.

"Hello. I'm told this is my first class."

He was gorgeous by any measure—clean-cut auburn hair, bright green eyes, a strong jawline, and an athletic build. A buzz rippled through the classroom. The girls wanted to know more, and the boys were annoyed at the presence of new competition.

The boy handed a note to Mr. Gilbert, who welcomed

him to the class. "Okay, Will. Boy, we're getting a number of new kids late in the year here. Will Rasch, go ahead and introduce yourself to the class."

With a smoldering stare, he faced the group. "My name it Will Rasch. I only arrived in Clear Lake this morning. This is my first day." His eyes settled on Vickie, who stared intently at him and concentrated as hard as she could. The feeling in her stomach spread to her whole body when he looked at her, and she tapped her toes involuntarily.

He took a seat in the back of the classroom. From the front, Vickie could sense his eyes boring into the back of her head. She even scratched it a few times because she was so uncomfortable.

Irritated, she spun to look at him again. He simply stared at her and made no effort to look anywhere else. He had a similar look of determined concentration on his face.

"Hey, Vickie, take a picture, will you?" The boy seated behind her chuckled.

"Miss Hewitt, is there anything more important in the back of the class that you'd like to share with us?" Mr. Gilbert flashed her an annoyed look as she spun to face him again.

"No, sir. Sorry."

He nodded and continued the lesson.

She squirmed in her seat throughout the entire hour and tried everything she could to calm herself. Unfortunately, nothing worked. The nervous energy pulsed through her stomach and her limbs to make her antsy and distracted.

Finally, the bell rang to end the hour. She hunched

forward and held her head in her hands. *You're going crazy. No, you're not. Yes, you are. What is happening? Are you losing your mind? Your senses? Get it under control. But get what under control? I don't even know what's happening.*

She raised her head and stood to draw the backpack straps over her shoulders. After a long, slow breath, she turned to head to the door and startled involuntarily. Will still sat in his desk and watched her intently.

"What?" she asked.

He shook his head without saying anything, then stood and walked out ahead of her.

Alexis waited for Vickie outside the classroom. She stared at Will when he walked past and down the hall.

"Whoa. Who's the babe?" she asked with a laugh.

"I...I don't know. But there's something wrong with him."

"Like what? He's too good-looking?" The two of them strolled side by side.

"No." Vickie stared at the floor. "I don't know what it is. But you know that feeling I had this morning? It got worse when he walked in. He's giving me some weird vibe, and it is making me really uncomfortable."

Alexis laughed. "Are you sure it's not a romantic vibe? Like, you want that piece of meat? Look at him. He's perfect"

"No, it's not that. I don't know what it is, but I know it's not that."

"How do you feel now?"

Vickie rubbed her stomach. "A little better now that he's gone. But I can't shake the feeling that something bad will happen. And based on how my body reacted, I think whatever it is will involve him."

Alexis shook her head. *It has to be the good-looking ones. That guy is gorgeous. I've never seen a more handsome boy in the halls of this school...maybe ever.*

I wonder what his story is.

CHAPTER TWENTY-FOUR

"So, you've never been bowling before, Vickie?" Jamie bent over to tie her sneakers while the other girls grabbed their coats.

It was the middle of the week. Often, just to mix it up, Alexis joined Jess and Jamie for a sleepover. They'd do something fun at night and go to school the next day. Everyone's parents were okay with the arrangement, provided they were not late to school in the morning.

This time, they all stayed at Jamie's house south of the high school. Vickie was invited to join them.

"I'm not even sure what bowling is." She giggled while she zipped her jacket.

"It's easy—you throw a ball and you knock things down." Alexis patted her on the back. "The rules are simple. Plus, this is mini bowling. It's even easier. You'll see."

Jamie said goodbye to her parents, and she pushed open the creaky screen door attached to the front of the bunga-low. The four girls skipped down the steps and walked up the sidewalk.

They rotated who hosted these little get-togethers, but Jamie's was usually the most fun because they were able to do an unsupervised Girls' Night Out.

"Remember, girls, curfew is 10 pm." Jamie walked backward to speak to the group. "That means we have about three hours to knock out a few games and get back here. I don't want to sprint down the sidewalk like last time."

"We made it back." Jess laughed. "Besides, I was on a roll. If I get into that same groove again, I make no guarantees about getting back in time for curfew."

"What does curfew mean?" Vickie tugged on Alexis' shoulder.

"It means you get in trouble if you're under the age of seventeen and you're out without an adult. We'll be fine, though. Koz's is right up the road here on the left."

Light rain sprinkled the girls' heads while they marched to Koz's Mini Bowl. The establishment was a Milwaukee staple—a small bar barely large enough to fit more than twenty people at a time.

Since they were minors, the girls were not there to hang out at the bar. They wanted to bowl.

Past the bar area was a small back room that held four mini bowling lanes. It was an old-fashioned hangout that Milwaukee residents had enjoyed for decades.

And it was only a short walk from Jamie's house.

As they approached the big Koz's sign, Alexis spoke to the group. "Ladies, don't make eye contact with anyone in the bar area besides the bartender. Go straight to the back and let's stay out of trouble. I don't want to have anyone arrested tonight. I want to knock down some pins." The girls cheered with excitement. Vickie joined them, despite not really knowing how any of this worked yet.

They walked up the few steps and into the small bar. Despite being popular, the owners of Koz's rarely performed any updates to the building itself. This was by design. The charm of Koz's Mini Bowl was that it felt like an old-timey bar from decades before.

A wave of excitement surged over Alexis. She always loved Girls' Night Out at Koz's. Something about walking into a bar without any parental supervision made a girl feel like she was an independent adult.

As instructed, the friends marched through the bar area to a podium at the back of the room. Beyond the podium, three of the four mini bowling lanes were in use. They were assigned lane two and took a scorecard with a pencil.

"Why did you take that?" Alexis asked Jamie. "You know we won't actually use it. I'll just open the app on my phone."

"Why can't we use the paper? It's an old-fashioned place so you might as well enjoy all the old-fashioned...ness of it."

"None of us know how to keep score, that's why." Alexis pulled up a bowling scorecard app and punched in everyone's names. "I'll go first, then Jess, Jamie, and Vickie." She winked at the vampire. "I put you at the end so you can watch us do our thing first. You should be able to pick it up in no time."

"I hope so."

Koz's had no bowling shoes, so everyone wore their sneakers. Minutes later, they each had a mini bowling ball and they were set up to play.

Alexis picked up her sparkling purple ball, walked to

the line, and rolled it as hard as she could. When it reached the pins, it struck with a loud, explosive sound, but three pins remained standing.

"Tough break," Jess said. "It sounded good, though."

At the other end of the lane, an older teenage boy scrambled to pick up the fallen pins and clear the way for her to take another shot. After launching her ball down the lane one more time, she managed to knock down two of the remaining three pins. She sat beside Vickie while the others bowled.

"So you get two shots?"

"Two shots. And don't bother to try to use your powers on me now. I'm onto you. Play like a human."

Outwardly, Vickie laughed and rolled her eyes. But inside? *Yes, I get it. I'm not a human. I need to act like one. Stop being a vampire. Blah blah blah.*

Koz's held to an old bowling tradition of having human pinsetters. While the big chain bowling alleys implemented machinery that set up pins for you automatically, Koz's stationed four people—usually older teenagers—behind the lanes. Between shots, they rushed to retrieve the fallen pins and set the next shot up quickly. It was a job worked at a furious pace, but it added a little extra charm to the tiny bowling alley.

Jamie bowled her frame and told Vickie it was her turn. While she walked back to her seat, she looked at the dozens of people crammed into the bar area.

"Can you imagine if there was a fire?" Alexis asked with wide eyes. "I know it's part of the charm, but it can't be safe."

"Shoot, what about smoking? Smoking is illegal indoors now. If this bar didn't have that rule—"

"We probably wouldn't be able to see the pins."

Vickie picked up a bright pink ball, barely larger than a honeydew melon, reared back, and whipped it down the lane like a gunshot. The ball catapulted the pins and not only knocked them down but obliterated any sense of structure. The targets flew so hard that some of them ended up on the other lanes.

The entire staff at the far end rushed to restore order. Pins had landed everywhere and some still spun on their sides.

"That's good, right? I'm supposed to knock them down." She gave her friends a thumbs-up.

Alexis waved her over. "Let me take a shot and then we'll talk about what happened back there." This time, she picked up the spare ball and walked back to where Vickie sat.

"Did I hit them too hard?"

"Oh yeah."

"Should I back off a little bit?"

"Just a smidge."

The vampire nodded and kept the advice in mind while she watched the other girls bowl. She stood from the chair and chose the pink ball again.

"Hey, Vickie, what's the latest on Eric?" Jess asked.

I guess she really isn't that jealous of someone trying to be with Eric. "It's going fine, I guess. I don't really know. I'm simply trying to be in his life so that, when he's ready, all he has to do is show up." She then proceeded to explain the cross country situation over Homecoming Weekend.

"That's…kind of brilliant, actually," Jess said. "Way to go."

Vickie hurled the ball down the lane, but this time, it connected solidly with the front pin to knock all the others down in the process.

The girls cheered her on. "My first strike."

"Anyway, I think you should ask him." Jess smiled at her. "Come on. Girls do it all the time now. Don't be so old-fashioned that you wind up alone on Homecoming Weekend because you didn't have the courage to speak up and ask."

That's a good point. But where is the line? How do I figure out where that point might be? Change the subject. I don't want to talk about this right now.

She opened her mouth to see if she could distract them with another topic. But before she could say anything, Jamie jumped in and asked the group an important question.

"What do you think of the new guy?"

The girls swooned and stared off into space while they pictured themselves dating the dreamboat. All the girls except Vickie.

"He is so cute. He could work in Hollywood."

"I hope he asks me out."

That last sentence shook Vickie somewhat. She still wasn't sure why she felt so weird about this boy, but it was very clear the other girls were infatuated.

"His hair."

"His jawline."

"Those eyes!"

They all spent several minutes listing his individual features while Vickie begged them to bowl.

"Come on, please? Let's go. I don't want to sit and talk about a boy all night."

"Don't you like him, Vickie?" Jess asked. "He's so cute, I think he could be on TV if he wanted to."

"No, I'm not a fan. I don't know why, but he rubs me the wrong way." She sneered and finished it with a grimace.

"Where is he from?" Jamie asked the group and continued to ignore Vickie's negative comments.

"Somebody said he was from Europe," Alexis stated. "I don't know where, though. But what are the odds of that, hey, Vickie? I think it's kinda cool. And he could be from someplace really romantic, like Paris."

Jess walked over and picked her ball up. "I think it's crazy how many international students we have this year. It seems like every week, we have a new one."

Alexis nodded. "Especially from China. I can think of three from China right off the bat."

"But what would they want in Clear Lake?" Jamie twisted her face in confusion.

"Who knows? I can't understand what draws men anywhere, but then what do I know? I never thought of Clear Lake as being much of an international high school, but it totally is now."

The girls bowled with new enthusiasm and squeezed in three full games before it was time to go home for the day.

They stepped onto the sidewalk again and set off quietly for home. The light drizzle had turned into heavier rain and they had to get back to Jamie's as soon as possible.

"Once we get there, we can order more food or eat from the cupboards or what? We only had to be at home for the curfew."

The group agreed to explore the cupboards of Jamie's kitchen to find enough food to get them through the evening.

That night, Vickie hoped that maybe they would call Eric on the phone and he could ask her to Homecoming. *It would've been super-lame, but at least something would have happened that mattered.*

Bowling was fun, but she was still preoccupied with Eric and whether or not she would go to Homecoming.

The friends marched up the front steps of the house at 9:54 pm. They had made curfew, and they spent the rest of the night not sleeping but instead, playing games and generally goofing around.

At one point, Vickie sat back and smiled at her new friends. As weird as they seemed to be in that moment, it provided yet another time for her to appreciate being a human instead of a vampire.

CHAPTER TWENTY-FIVE

The next day—after the girls actually did make it to school on time—Vickie was on high alert. The new boy, Will, still gave her a strange feeling of trepidation that she could not explain. It didn't help that all the girls did the previous night was talk about how cute he was. He seemed to have a strange power over them that she could neither explain nor understand.

And yet, nothing changed. He spent algebra class staring at her. She spent the class feeling like a bundle of nerves around him. When that finally ended, he simply stood and left the room, and everyone went about their day.

Despite his odd connection to Vickie, he didn't go out of his way to say anything to her. He didn't confront her and seemed content to simply watch her. She was too uncomfortable to approach him, as his presence continued to be very unsettling. Still, she was sure something was up with him.

"Maybe it's only your imagination." Alexis tried to calm

her between classes. "Things are going well for you so far. Don't spend all your time looking for reasons to ruin it. Enjoy what you have right now. High school doesn't always reward good people, so we have to savor it when it happens."

Like many typical teenage girls, Alexis didn't want to admit that something was wrong with the new, cute boy. She was infatuated with his good looks and smoldering gaze. Add to that a touch of mystery, and he was the perfect storm for a high school crush. If he turned out to be a bad guy in some way, she would be crushed.

Fortunately for both girls, Will had second lunch. Vickie didn't have to deal with him, and Alexis could stare at him from afar. He ate by himself, anyway.

When Vickie arrived at first lunch, she knew he wouldn't be around, which gave her much-needed relief. *At least I won't lose my appetite with that weirdo staring at me. What is his deal, anyway?*

To her surprise, there was a longer line for the food than usual. When she ran into Eric, she asked what the reason was.

"It's Build Your Own Pasta Bowl Day," he explained. "It only happens every once in a while, so it's really popular when we get it. I dropped our stuff off at the table while Jess got in line. She's holding a place for me. Come join us." He skipped off to join their friend who waved him over.

Vickie was ready to join them, but she noticed the line for drinks was nonexistent. On her way to the table, she bought a plastic container of white milk. It was a little bigger than the carton, and she was very thirsty for some reason.

She brought it over to their usual place, dropped her bag on her chair, and placed the milk on the table before she headed into the line to get her pasta.

All the other kids pushed and shoved, eager to grab their lunches.

"I've never seen them all so excited for lunch," she observed as she tried to stay upright. "This feels like a riot."

"Last year, they actually ran out of pasta," Eric said. "It was a huge deal."

Jess nodded. "Yep. And the principal announced they would make sure an error like that would never happen again. But because it happened once, everyone thinks it could happen anytime. That's why these lines are so long and aggressive."

They finally reached the food line on the other side of the wall and grabbed their trays. A few minutes later, they emerged with bowls of noodles smothered in tomato and meat sauce and doughy garlic breadsticks on the side.

Vickie was excited. *This looks delicious. And of all the things people get wrong about vampires, I'm glad one of them is the garlic thing. I can't wait to eat these breadsticks. Now, it would break my heart to not be able to eat garlic.*

"You got your drink already?" Eric pointed to the small container on the table. "Nice work."

"I saw an opening, so I took it." Vickie set her tray down on the table. "Now look at the line."

Because everyone got their pasta first, the milk line was now growing. "Shoot!" Eric said and shook his head. He put his tray down and jogged over to get in line for milk.

Vickie watched him jog away, then smirked at Jess. "You know, I thought you two were dating."

She scoffed at the idea. "Oh, man. No. No way. Me and Eric? Not a chance."

"That's what Alexis said."

"Eric is like my brother. I love him but I would never want to get anywhere near dating him."

The vampire frowned, both concerned and a little confused. "Why is that? Is there something wrong with him?"

"No, no, that's not why. He's simply not my type. And that's all right. I hope he finds somebody who likes him a lot and would treat him right." She nodded at Vickie. "That would make me very happy for him. He's great. He deserves a good girlfriend."

Vickie blushed at the unspoken hint, and the two girls clammed up quickly once Eric returned to the table. "The line wasn't so bad. It moved fast."

For a few minutes, everybody prepared their meal and tore open packets of Parmesan cheese to sprinkle it over their pasta and sauce. They mixed their creations together and began to eat.

"Wow, this is really good." Vickie was pleasantly surprised. "I guess it lives up to the hype."

Eric laughed. "It's sad that noodles with sauce is such an upgrade for this cafeteria, but it is."

As she chewed, another wave of uncertainty surged over her. She looked around the room. *That Will guy isn't in here, is he? He has the other lunch, so he should be in class.* The sickening feeling was still strong, however, and dragged her down to earth just as she was enjoying the pasta and the good company.

She shook her head and tried her best to not pay attention to it while she reached for her milk. The feeling intensified, but nothing she saw explained it.

Unfortunately for her, it's what she didn't see that made the difference.

Megan Fitz was in the same lunch period. While seated at her table, Megan had seen Vickie put her container of milk and backpack on the table and leave them there.

With devilish glee, she scanned her thoughts on what would be a great way to embarrass the girl. As very few people actually paid attention, she walked over to the milk, opened the container's screw cap, and dumped an entire salt shaker into it. She replaced the cap and tightened it as hard as she could so that it looked like it hadn't been opened.

Before she left it, she shook it to distribute the salt evenly throughout the milk. After that, it was merely a matter of waiting. *This will be great. If she thought she was embarrassed before...*

Vickie returned to the table with her tray of pasta and sat with her friends. At her table, Megan tapped a few girls on their shoulders and pointed in her direction. "Watch this."

When the milk hit her lips, Vickie knew something was wrong. She was so thirsty, she continued to drink and actually swallowed several gulps before the horrible taste kicked in.

Fire burned down her throat and in every nook and cranny of her mouth. In the middle of the swig, she instinctively spat the milk in her mouth across the table and directly into Eric's face.

Her eyes were as wide as dinner plates while most of the kids burst into laughter at the horrible situation.

Vickie's stomach dropped. "Eric. I'm so sorry."

Milk dripped from his chin and his ears and soaked his shirt. It ran off the tip of his nose and onto the plate of pasta in front of him. Even though he kept his lips tightly closed in disgust at what had happened, he tried not to be visibly grossed out by it. He took a deep breath to keep himself from reacting. *She didn't mean to do it. Obviously, something is wrong. She wouldn't do that to you on purpose. Look how mortified she is that this even happened. Don't make her feel bad about it.*

He waved it off. "It was an accident. What's going on with you?"

"I don't know. It was the milk. There was something wrong with it and— I honestly don't know. It tasted awful and my body naturally kicked it out."

Megan walked past and laughed cockily at the mess that was created. "You need to be more careful, little girl. That is very bad manners."

Her. It was her. Get her now. Vickie pushed to her feet and grabbed her container of milk before she gave chase. Halfway around the cafeteria room, the girl stopped to regard her with a smug grin.

"Is something wrong with your milk, darling?" Her voice dripped with condescension.

"You did this. I don't know what you have against me, but you did something to my milk." By comparison, the vampire's voice was tinged with anger.

"I really don't know what you're talking about."

Vickie's rage bubbled up again and coursed through her

body. She placed her hand on Megan's face and shoved her. She merely wanted to send her a message but forgot how strong she was, especially when angry.

That little shove slammed Megan Fitz violently to the floor where she bumped her head forcefully on the tile. She clutched the back of her head in pain and immediately sat up. All the activity in the cafeteria froze when half the student body and its faculty witnessed the incident.

Vickie paid no attention to any of it. She had become blind with anger. *Do something to her. Anything, but don't injure her. Embarrass her and do it in front of everyone, exactly like she did to you.*

She opened the container of salty milk and dumped it all over her enemy, who screamed. Audible gasps were heard from the onlookers, who couldn't believe what they witnessed.

Megan seemed close to tears. The white milk covered her blouse and her face, and it was even in her hair. She stood, dazed but upright. The milk ran down her legs and soaked into her shoes. Then her knees buckled, and she fell once more.

Like Muhammad Ali standing over Sonny Liston in the iconic photo, Vickie crowed over Megan and glared at her with rage. Before she could try her hand at trash talk, she was accosted by the vice principal, who pulled her away for a chat.

"Excuse me, young lady, but this is not how we handle things here." He was stern and clearly tried to contain his temper. His face had gone beet red and his small mustache appeared to glow against the contrast of his darkened skin.

"Somebody stole the—"

"I don't care. We do not inflict bodily harm on one another. For that, you will apologize to her and you will also serve time in detention. I have a zero-tolerance policy for violence in my school, and you disobeyed that."

With as much insincerity as she could cram into an apology, Vickie looked at the dejected bully and said, "Sorry."

Megan's friends rallied to her side to help her up and walk her to the bathroom. "Let's get you cleaned up. It's okay. It's over." Megan sobbed while she limped out of the room.

Vickie felt satisfied with her work, but when she looked around the cafeteria, she realized that Megan wasn't the one embarrassed. Instead, everyone continued to stare at her.

The retaliation had felt good in the moment, but it did nothing to help her reputation.

The principal wrote her a note so that she would know when and where to go for detention.

A few hours later, Alexis talked to Vickie about her day but seemed distracted and only half paid attention. But when Vickie mentioned to her that she had obtained revenge on Megan Fitz, she cheered. "That will show her. I wish I had been there for that. She deserved every last drop. And you know what? I heard someone had done something to Megan, but nobody seemed to have any details. That is so great. What did you do?" *She's standing up for herself. I love it.*

"I shoved her to the ground, and she hit her head."
Uh oh. "Vickie…"

"And then I dumped an entire container of milk over her."

"Was she hurt?"

"I don't know. They helped her out of the room. I didn't hear anything, so I assume she's fine now."

"Well…that's a little more extreme than I had thought. But as long as she's okay. We don't want to injure anyone." *I keep forgetting about her strength when she panics. I hope she didn't hurt her on purpose.*

"I have detention, though. I don't even know what that is."

"It's fine. My dad will probably give you a speech about how disappointed he is in you. You have to stay after school, sit in a room, and think about what you did. It's not a big deal at all. What's important is that you stood up for yourself and you didn't kill her. That is so awesome. And that's how you shut down a bully."

Vickie straightened and smiled. She still had detention, but at least she was proud. She'd shut Megan Fitz up—for the time being, anyway.

CHAPTER TWENTY-SIX

The halls were almost empty. At the end of the school day, most students rushed out of the building like their hair was on fire.

But in Room 105, a small handful of students sat in detention, led by Mr. Gilbert, of all people.

At first, Vickie was happy to see him. He seemed to like having her as a student. *At least the guy running it will be nice to me.* She flashed him a smile when she walked in but was met with a stern, unhappy face. *Maybe not.*

Once everyone was there, he heaved his ample frame out of the chair and closed the door to the classroom. Then, he walked to the front of the room. "Good afternoon. This is detention. This is not playtime, phone time, or talking time. For the next hour, you will sit in the desk you are seated in. You will not do homework. You will not play on your phones. And you definitely will not socialize. This is a punishment and we expect you to receive it that way." He sat at the desk in front of the classroom again and immediately fell asleep, his arms folded across the top of his belly.

That's it? We simply sit here? Who else is in here, anyway? It looks like Craig and Chris are both here. Oh, and there's April. Most of the troublemakers, I guess. It's funny how I get pranked and I'm the one who gets punished. How fair is that?

She worried that she would struggle to pass the time, but her memory relieved her. *Vickie, you spent four hundred years awake in a box with nothing to do. You can sit at this desk for an hour and entertain yourself.*

Despite her ability to pass the time, detention still seemed irritatingly long to her. Being awake and adjusting to life as a teenager had spoiled her somewhat. She hadn't waited for anything for the last few months, and now, she was forced to slow down again.

She passed the time by looking around the room, wondering what each of the other kids was in for. Bringing drugs to school? Getting into a fistfight? Disrespecting teachers? Not coming to class?

After she exhausted all those possibilities, she stared at the photo timeline hanging in the front of the class that listed all the United States Presidents. She remembered studying them for her initial testing, so she quizzed herself on little facts about each President and tested herself as to whether she could still list them in order from memory.

So this is what boredom feels like. Wow. This is brutal. Still, it was so sweet to shove Megan and humiliate her like that. I can't believe she made me spit my milk into Eric's face. The poor boy. I wanted to help him, but I didn't know how. I bet I lost any chance of a date with him. How do you get romantic with someone who spat milk all over your face? I feel like that would be a deal-breaker for him. Stupid Megan. She deserved what she got from me.

And on that note, she leaned back in her desk and relived the scene a few hundred times in a row and smiled every single time.

Once detention was over, Vickie walked out the front door of the building and was picked up by Craig. She'd missed cross country practice thanks to the punishment. Not that she needed practice, but she wanted to continue to be an active member of the team so missing practice was a bummer.

When he pulled up in the SUV, she climbed into the passenger seat and fastened her seat belt without saying a word. Craig pressed the gas pedal and merged back into traffic, his teeth gritted.

"I'm really disappointed in you, Vickie," he said and immediately filled the prediction Alexis had given her. "Explain what happened. I want to hear your side of it."

"Megan Fitz keeps embarrassing me in front of everyone."

"How?"

"She concocted a plan to get me stood up on a date at Johnny V's in front of everyone. And today, she dumped salt in my milk, which made me spew it all over the table and all over Eric. It was humiliating. She tries constantly to embarrass me, and she does a really good job of it."

Craig kept his eyes on the road and stared intently ahead while he tried to think of what to say. *This is your first opportunity to discipline the poor girl. Don't screw it up. You know how to talk to Alexis. Choose your words carefully here.* "Why do you let her get to you?"

"What do you mean?" Vickie folded her arms and looked at him, her expression a little wounded.

"When she plays a prank on you, do you react? Do you get mad, or sad? Do you give her an emotional response?"

"Of course." Vickie shrugged. "I don't like it when these things happen to me."

"I've learned over the years that bullies really only want to get a reaction out of someone. If you don't react to it, you rob them of the satisfaction of whatever it is they're trying to do to you. The payoff to the prank is your reaction. So stop reacting and they'll stop pranking."

Vickie looked out the window. *It makes sense, I guess. But how do you not react when you spit milk all over the guy you like? Or are stood up in front of everyone?* "These pranks are really stiff. They're public, in front of the entire student body, and they hurt. How do I not react to any of those?"

"My dad taught me how to do it." He smirked. "He explained the same thing I did to you—your reaction is the payoff. So, sometimes I would laugh at the joke. At other times, I wouldn't react at all. My job was to make sure that I didn't get mad or sad. Those two emotions were blood in the water for bullies."

"Were you ever bullied?"

"Oh yeah. But back then, they didn't call it bullying. Some kids were jerks and others weren't. We didn't take it as seriously but the pranks were still there. You're familiar with bubbler rides?"

"Alexis explained them to me, yes. What about them?"

Craig sighed. "When I was a freshman in high school, the older members of the football team really had it in for me. They sabotaged my food—or simply ate it outright.

Sometimes, they threw my books in the trash. Stupid stuff. Well, one day, they gave me a bubbler ride. The front of my pants was soaked to the bone, underwear and all."

"Ugh."

"Oh yeah. And they'd do it in the middle of the morning, too. That way, I wouldn't be able to sneak home and change my pants. So I was stuck in really wet clothes that stuck to my skin all day. Not very comfortable."

"Why is this related to what I'm going through?"

"Hang on, I'm getting there. I hated that bubbler ride but I did it. I took it without complaint. They hated that about me. They'd try to prank me, but I never let them see that I was bothered by it. They grew determined—as in laser-focused—to get me to crack."

"What did they do?" Vickie sat up straight.

"They gave me bubbler rides every day. Every day. Without fail. And when that didn't work, they'd spray your butt instead. But I kept quiet. They bumped it up to twice a day. They were determined to beat back this resolve in me. But I wouldn't let them. I walked around for two weeks with endlessly soaked clothes. And I never got mad at them."

"Wow." Vickie looked at the floor. "I'm surprised you didn't have more issues with your clothing if it was constantly wet."

"That wasn't the worst of it, either. I was also victim to the longest wedgie in history. They cornered me in the locker room—before practice of course—and lifted me off the ground about two feet, only hanging onto my underwear. The fabric stretched and stretched and eventually ended up higher than my head."

"Did you scream then?"

"Nope. I bit my tongue. I watched the elastic double and triple in size right before my very eyes."

"I'm surprised it didn't rip."

"That's actually what they planned. But because I wore fairly new underwear, they didn't rip. The guys had a section of the locker room with a hook on it. It was near the ceiling, and they stacked waistbands on it. It was like their own little ghetto trophy case, except nobody actually wants to watch that. It stayed in the locker room."

"And they never got their trophy from you?"

"I'm sure they enjoyed seeing me go out for a run with my waistband hiked up past my chest. That was probably payment enough for all the torture I had to go through." Another beat of silence settled around them. *Bring it home, Craig.* "Vickie, you need to keep yourself in control. If you can do that, they can't beat you in anything. You will win the war. When they try to embarrass you, feel embarrassed for them instead. You're a vampire, so keeping your emotions in check is a big honking deal."

When they reached home again, Vickie stared out at the pool. "When can we use this thing?"

"Anytime you want. It's only a little dirty at the bottom." Craig walked over to the pool to show her the liner and how to roll it up. "Besides," he explained, "we'll close it up soon, so you might as well get some time in there before it's too late."

He walked toward the house but she remained where she was. He paused and looked at her for a moment. "Do you understand what I'm trying to tell you about the bullies?"

"They have no power over me."

"Exactly." *Nailed it. She knows what I'm rambling about.* "Please, no more inflicting bodily harm and injury on some of these people. Stay quiet. Laugh at yourself if you must. But don't let them see how you really feel. There's an old saying, 'Sticks and stones may break my bones, but words can never hurt me.'"

Vickie waved him off to stare at the pool for a few more minutes before she turned and headed inside. The air was a little too cold to simply stand out there. Now that she'd served her time and inflicted a little fear into Megan Fitz, she felt she could return to school on Monday and be confident that no one would mess with her anymore.

CHAPTER TWENTY-SEVEN

Lunch on Monday was a little more low-key. Vickie arrived and dropped her bag at the table before she joined the food line. As chance would have it, Megan Fitz stood directly in front of her.

Oh, great. The last thing I need is another fight with her. Please don't bother me today, Megan. I honestly want a day without any drama.

Neither of them spoke. In fact, neither of them even looked at each other. The other girl watched her out of the corner of her eye, and the tension between them was thick, but nothing happened.

But as in most situations Vickie had been in since she'd started high school at Clear Lake, all eyes were on her. She didn't care for so much attention all the time, but she had built a reputation for her share of drama.

As she carried her tray to the table, her classmates watched her carefully.

She practically slammed her tray down and sat in her

seat. The impact made Eric jump, a little defensive from the previous day's events.

"Is there a problem?" Jess asked and looked at her a little warily.

Vickie rubbed her temples. "I simply want to be normal. Is that too much to ask? Can't I blend in and live my life without everyone watching me?"

Her friend chewed and swallowed a bite of her sandwich. "No offense, but when you shove a girl down and dump milk all over her, you basically give up the chance to blend in with the rest of the class. That's on you."

She took a bite of her pizza. "I know. I just… I feel like I get cornered into this stuff. I don't want to be this person."

"If it makes you feel any better, Megan Fitz seems terrified of you now." Jess pointed to the other girl's table. She watched Vickie but this time, she didn't smile.

Good. That does make me feel a little better. One less thing to worry about around here. "Well, that was the point. I hope it sticks. We're only a few weeks into school and I'm already tired of her." She looked at Eric. "How are you?"

"I'm okay. How's your pizza? Did you try your milk yet?"

Vickie laughed. "I won't spew all over you again like that. Don't worry. I'm really sorry. Listen, I have something for you—why don't we meet after school today? We can walk to practice together and I can give it to you."

"Oooh…" Jess sang under her breath.

"Not like that." The vampire shot her an annoyed glance. Eric laughed nervously.

After her last class of the day, she walked to her locker.

On her way, she crossed paths with Megan yet again. Both of them stopped in the hallway to stare at one another.

All the self-confidence and cocky swagger that Megan had oozed when they had first met was gone. In its place was a frightened little girl who didn't know whether to stand up to Vickie or run away screaming.

Vickie held the power, and she liked it.

Megan's friends pushed her along. "Leave her be. You don't need to mess with that."

The vampire tossed her backpack in her locker and retrieved a small gift bag. When she turned, Eric already waited for her with a smile on his face.

"Hey."

"Hey. I got you this."

Eric took the bag from her and peeked inside. "You really didn't have to do this. The whole thing was an accident. This is unnecessary." He tried to hand her the bag back, but she refused.

"That's yours. I have no use for it. I only hope I got the right size."

He pulled out a light-blue t-shirt, similar to the one he had worn the previous day when she showered him with milk. "I love it. This is great, it really is. I've had a hard time cleaning the last one anyway because the milk soaked into it all afternoon. Now, I can simply toss it and wear this one instead. You're the best."

Vickie blushed. *You did the right thing, girl. Keep it up.*

They walked shoulder to shoulder down the hallways to the locker rooms on the other side of the school building. Alexis and Jamie caught their eyes and smiled warmly.

"Woo hoo," they teased.

"Shut up," Eric shouted back. "You're being lame."

But when Vickie looked at Eric, she saw his flushed cheeks. He avoided eye contact with her too. He was definitely self-conscious around her. Alexis had explained to Vickie that this was a good sign. It meant he probably liked her.

They had almost reached the locker room area when Coach Lueck shouted out from his desk in the classroom. "Hey, Vickie. Can you come in here for a minute?"

"I'll wait." Eric stood faithfully outside the door. Even though the locker room entrance was a few steps away, he would wait for her to walk with him. *What a gentleman. I didn't think there even were gentlemen around here in this day and age. That's a nice little bonus.*

Coach reviewed a few notes on his desk when he waved her in. "Hurry. I wanted to talk to you before the rest of the team comes in."

"What can I do for you, Coach?"

He looked up from his notes. "You ran one heck of a race last week. I was really impressed, and I didn't know what to expect out of you. You started out slow, though."

Vickie nodded. *That's because I didn't want to leave everyone in my dust in my very first race, sir.* "Well, I'm not used to racing yet, sir. I was still feeling out pacing and all the things I could do better."

He nodded slowly, then propped his elbows on his knees, folded his hands, and tucked them under his chin. "So here's where I'm at, Vickie. With your race time, you are a shoo-in for the Varsity team. I want to put you on Varsity yesterday. That's how good I think you can be. I think you have real raw talent that we can turn into a runner who can anchor this team and win you a whole lot of medals."

"That sounds great. But what's the problem?"

He sighed. "You don't have a whole lot of racing experience here. If you go out too slow in a Varsity race, you might not be able to recover so easily. That's all I'm saying. I think you can be an asset to the Varsity team, but only if you can get your pacing under control. Can you run smarter? If I put you on Varsity, will it be a mistake? Do you think you can step up?"

She nodded enthusiastically. "Of course I can. I can jump onto the team and help lead it. I really can, I promise. You won't see problems like that again in the future."

He straightened and scrutinized her one more time. "Okay. Let's do it. Let's put you on the Varsity team."

Vickie clapped with excitement and shook his hand. "All right, now go get ready for practice. You're training with Varsity now. Gotta be ready."

She ran out of the room with her arms outstretched toward Eric. "I just made Varsity."

He cheered his support, and the two of them embraced. But rather than break the hug immediately like friends would do, they lingered a few seconds longer. Both realized it, but neither of them wanted to say it. They enjoyed it too much.

Finally, they released.

"My heart is fluttering right now." Vickie patted her chest. "He says I have a lot of raw talent and if I can settle my pacing, I could be a strong runner for the Varsity team."

"That is so cool. Hey, that means you could go to Minnesota if you wanted to."

"That's right."

Eric paused for a second to watch her expression. "Do you want to?"

"What?"

"Go to Minnesota. You know, on that trip. Do you want to go to that? Or would you rather stay here for Homecoming?"

"I guess…" She trailed off. "I would approach it the same way you are. If I have a date to Homecoming, then I'll go. But if not…"

"You'd go to Minnesota?"

"Yeah."

"So which would you rather do?"

She thought about it for a second. *If I go to Minnesota, I'll have all kinds of time with Eric. It would be really cool, and it could be a whole weekend together. If I go to Homecoming, it would be a night together. But Alexis would also be there to guide me, and I know I still need her help. Boy, this is tough.*

"It's my first Homecoming. I would really like to go to the dance. But I think either would be a lot of fun."

Eric nodded as if he'd made a mental note. "Yeah, I know what you mean. It's an interesting problem to have. I only hope we don't have to deal with this sort of thing again next year."

They walked past the entrance to the girls' locker room. Vickie smiled at him and stepped inside. *I hope he doesn't pick the Minnesota trip after all this. If he does, will I seem too obvious if I go along, too? Ugh, I hate all this waiting around.*

She rounded the corner and was greeted by cheers from the other girls. "What's up?" she asked in confusion.

Krista walked up and put her arm around Vickie. "Coach says you'll be on the Varsity team now."

That was quick. He just talked to me.

"He talked to Shannon first, and she gave the okay."

This was a relief to Vickie. Alexis had told her she needed to get along with her teammates. And while Krista had been a great supporter of hers, she didn't really know how the rest of the team felt about her. One of the reasons she didn't want to run too fast was that she didn't want to make the other teammates feel threatened. They worked hard to get where they were, and she was simply there because running was part of her being.

To know that she had the support of the team captain was a tremendous weight off her shoulders.

Shannon smiled while she tied her shoes. "You're a great runner, Vickie. We're excited to have you on our side. We need a fifth man to really anchor our team. We think you can do it."

The other Varsity girls high-fived Vickie, and she changed into her running clothes for her first Varsity-exclusive workout.

CHAPTER TWENTY-EIGHT

A stiff, cold wind blew across the empty reservoir in the middle of the night. Standing in the center of it, Vickie gazed at the full moon while she stretched her legs and craned her neck to peer into the clear night sky.

It was 2:00 am, and all was quiet in the neighborhood. All except the friendly neighborhood vampire who was out embracing her vampire powers under the cloak of night.

The moonlight reflected off the shiny tips on her fangs as she bared them. Few feelings comforted her like being able to freely open her mouth with her fangs in place.

Okay, Vickie. Aim for that tree. It's a few miles away, but it looks like I can scale it pretty quickly. Let's go.

In scant seconds, she had crossed several miles and sat on the top branch of a very tall tree. She straightened her faded white gown so it billowed around her feet to keep her whole body a little warmer.

Vickie stared at the full moon again. There was not a cloud in the sky. It was dark but impossibly bright at the same time.

Let's really kick it into gear.

She leapt down from the branch and burst into a sprint as she landed, her legs pumping as fast as they could. Maintaining her super-speed, she circled the reservoir a few times along the hill that surrounded it.

Dirt and dust kicked up into the air. She ran so quickly that some dust she'd displaced behind her actually caught her in the face the next time she circled.

It made her chuckle and slow. Finally, she stopped and spat out the dirt in her mouth. *It's not like running a lot makes you more of a vampire, Vickie. And running less doesn't mean you're less of a vampire. Times are changing. Relationships are changing. I've met a lot of new people and built an entirely new life.*

She liked coming out here and letting her vampire instincts take over. The problem was, it wasn't exactly fulfilling. She wanted to be a vampire—with other vampires. But she was the last one.

This little exercise she did kept the spirit alive, even if it was dying everywhere else she went.

Vickie thought back to sprinting in these kinds of fields with her brother and sister. They would run, jump, play tag, and do the little things that small kids liked to do when they had a few spare minutes.

That was one of the last things they did together. She smiled that the lasting memory she had of her siblings was of them running and playing—being kids and being happy.

There was something so innocent about that time. I could be a vampire and not really worry so much about who heard me. Before they took my siblings, we could simply exist. Then we had to go into hiding. That was the beginning of the end for me.

Keeping her vampire powers buried inside her was not easy. Fortunately, she had enough guidance to make it work. But when she was too overwhelmed by the ways of the world, she could go outside in the middle of the night and simply be.

It wasn't as freeing as some of the great times she had as a child, but those days had been long gone for years.

She ran back to the yard and walked carefully into the house. It was almost 3:00 am and she would have to be up in a few hours.

Vickie always tiptoed through the house when she wore her gown. She didn't want her new family to know how much she missed being a vampire. *They've been so helpful and so supportive. I can keep this to myself. It's not like I do it for very long.*

In the morning, she stumbled out of bed and, to her surprise, everyone else was up.

They all exchanged pleasantries. Alexis cooked French toast in their brand-new nonstick pan that Craig bought the previous afternoon. She wore a weird grin on her face like she knew something but couldn't talk about it.

"What?"

"What?"

"Why are you smiling?"

"I'm not. Am I smiling?"

"Yes, you are. What do you know?"

She flipped the toast in the pan. "I know nothing."

Vickie grumbled while she grabbed a plate with a couple of pieces of French toast on it. She stopped at the kitchen counter to bathe it in maple syrup, then sat at the table to eat.

Alexis continued to smile.

"Seriously, what is your deal?"

"I know something you don't know."

"What?"

"I can't tell you."

She cut off a piece of toast. "You're really annoying this morning."

Craig walked in and blinked a few times as if trying to convince his eyes that he was awake.

"Mornin'."

"Good morning. Do you know why Alexis is smiling so much?"

Craig took one look at his daughter and assumed he had the answer. "It must be a boy."

"Dad," Alexis protested with a hint of laughter. "It's not about a boy. There are no boys in my life right now."

"Then I got nothing." He squeezed Vickie's shoulder as he walked past to brew a cup of coffee for himself. The aroma alone was enough to kick everyone into gear along with the smells of breakfast that permeated the room.

When they arrived at school, Alexis' grin grew wider and wider. "Why are you in such a good mood already?" Vickie asked.

"What, I need a reason to be happy?" She unwrapped the piece of toast she carried.

"To be this happy, yeah."

"I simply know something you don't, that's all." She winked at her while she took a bite.

"Will I know about whatever this is? Like, soon?" The other girl simply shrugged and grinned around her mouthful. Vickie rolled her eyes. "I hate this."

They arrived at their normal meeting place in the halls of Clear Lake High School to a strange sight. Eric was awake.

"Wow, look at you—so alert this morning," Vickie joked.

Alexis was not surprised, however. "I gotta run to the library for a minute. Hey, girls, want to come?" Jess and Jamie stood and followed her, which left Vickie alone with Eric.

He looked unwell. His face was pale and he was sweating. His mouth seemed to be a little too dry. But he stood in front of Vickie and managed to hold his ground.

"Hey, so…I talked things over with the girls last night and this morning. We wanted to get a group together to go to Homecoming this year. It's kinda what we do every year."

Vickie smiled politely. She sensed she knew where the conversation was going, but she didn't want to get her hopes up.

"And Alexis said you would probably want to come with us. Is that right?" She nodded in response but tried hard not to look too eager. "So I…uh, wondered if you would like to kinda be my date for Homecoming. It doesn't have to be anything big. We would just…you know, be there together. Um, with everyone else."

Vickie felt like fireworks had erupted in her chest. She smiled brightly and accepted his invitation.

He released a huge sigh of relief. "Awesome. I'm really looking forward to it. I think it'll be fun."

"I do too. Were you really that nervous?"

"Oh yeah. Guys are usually nervous about this kind of

stuff." *That's an understatement, Eric. Your first time asking a girl out? Terrifying would be a better word.*

That's adorable. I thought I'd made it clear that I liked him ever since I got here. "Well, you don't have to worry about that anymore." She dropped her backpack beside his.

A few minutes later, the girls returned.

"Did you get what you needed at the library?" Vickie asked.

"They were...out of...stock," Alexis replied. "So we couldn't get anything. We'll have to try again sometime."

Vickie rose to her feet. "Can I have a word with you?" The two girls stepped away from the group and out into the main lobby. "You knew about this."

Alexis giggled loudly. "I sure did. Eric called me last night to ask if it was safe to ask you. I told him you were waiting for him to do that, and he said, 'Then I'll do it tomorrow.'"

Vickie nodded. "That is one good boy."

"I poked fun at him, like, 'You don't need my permission to ask her out.' But I know what he tried to do." She laughed again. "It's like he tried to propose to you or something. Although I know you wouldn't have had a problem with that."

Vickie slipped her hands in her pockets and leaned back to stretch her lower back. "How would this work, then? Can we still go with you guys?"

"Sure, why not? All that will change is seating arrangements. You can sit next to me and across from Eric. Then, whenever you hear something you don't know how to respond to, you can elbow me in the ribs or something. But make sure your temper is under control or you'll cave in my chest cavity."

"I doubt you have to worry about that. But what about you? What about your friendship with me and Eric? What happens to all that?" *I'm happy she's excited, but I still don't want to get in the way of their friendship. Then again, I already told him I would go, so if she suddenly changes her mind, I'm risking her friendship. Man, high school is complicated.*

Alexis smiled, then shook her head. *There's a reason I trusted this girl from day one. She cares, even if she doesn't understand it. That's a rare quality in a teenager.* "I learned a long time ago that good times and bad times don't last forever. If there's a breakup and something makes it awkward between you two, we'll have to ride that storm out before we can go any further as friends. And that's okay. I'd rather risk that than force you to not date simply because I'm worried about you breaking up."

The first bell rang, and the girls had to run back to their space and grab their backpacks. Vickie and Eric exchanged smiles, and everyone went their separate ways for the day.

Between classes, Vickie found Alexis and asked her a question that had been on her mind since she'd said yes to Eric—and even before. "What about getting you a date?"

I can think of a few. But we know that's a long shot. Don't put that pressure on her. She'll be worried enough about her own company that night. "I don't need a date, Vickie. Nobody needs a date. It would be nice, sure, but I don't need one to get by. I have my girls. You focus on having fun. It's only a dance."

Vickie nodded and continued to her next class. *She's*

right, but I still think it would be more fun if she had a date too. Maybe there's someone around here who would appreciate her company. She deserves to have some attention from the boys, too.

236

CHAPTER TWENTY-NINE

The girls changed back into their regular clothes after a tough Varsity practice. Krista's face was flushed and shiny, and she couldn't stop sweating as she paused mid-change to towel her dripping forehead repeatedly.

"Vickie, do you know what annoys me about you?"

"What?" *That's not a good way to open a conversation.*

"You don't sweat. Look at you. We all do everything we can to stop sweating like pigs, and you didn't sweat a drop during today's workout. Why is that?"

Think fast, Vickie. "I don't know. I...simply don't sweat. I've never been one to really sweat a whole lot."

That wasn't exactly true. Vickie did sweat in certain situations. But the workouts were not difficult for her and because they did not tax her body, it never overheated. Instead, she watched the expressions and behavior of the other runners and tried to mimic them as best she could.

That wasn't the only problem she had on Varsity, either. She could very easily outrun everyone on the team but that would bring attention to her. That was definitely not what she wanted despite the fact that she felt a spotlight had been on her this whole time so far.

So, instead of pacing herself with the girls in the front, she had to pace herself closer to the girls in the middle of the pack. It wasn't necessarily a bad thing, but it was a wrinkle she needed to work with. Trying to run slower required a lot more care and attention—and patience. Vickie didn't always have patience.

The other girls all said goodnight while she finished changing and packed her things up to go home. Craig was probably waiting for her so she couldn't waste much more time.

She slammed the locker shut and secured it with the padlock. When she walked out of the locker room, her stomach instantly dropped. *What was that? Why are you feeling like this? What's happening now?*

Vickie tried to shake the sensation and believed it would dissipate once she reached Craig's SUV and she could go home. All she needed to do was keep walking and she'd soon be out of the school and away from whatever had stirred the instincts she still didn't fully understand. She hurried around the corner and down the Social Studies Hall, then paused, caught by a compulsion she couldn't explain.

She spun to see if someone was watching her. Sure enough, down at the other end of the hall in the main lower lobby, was the new boy, Will.

He stood motionless, exactly like a statue. His entire body seemed frozen in the moment and his arms hung loosely at his sides. The focused, intense stare unnerved her. His head was slightly tilted to the right, and his face was expressionless, which seemed creepier if that were possible.

Despite the fact that she'd noticed him, he continued to regard her without even a trace of visible emotion.

"What?" she shouted and gestured dramatically with her arms. She received no response, only that empty, blank stare.

Vickie was tired of his apparently endless fascination with her, and she decided that moment was as good a time as any to confront him. She dropped her bags and marched down the hall to return his scrutiny as intently as he studied her.

"What?" she asked more forcefully as she approached him in the lower lobby. "What do you want?"

"I don't know," he replied.

I'm tired of feeling this way. I'm getting established in this new life and I don't need some weirdo to throw me off. It's time to get to the bottom of this. "What kind of answer is that? You've literally stared at me every day since you got here. Why are you doing this? What do you know?"

"I don't know," he replied again.

"What motivates you to stare at me and watch me? What is it about me that is so captivating to you? And don't say 'I don't know' again."

"When I see you, there is a spark."

Great. He's in love with me.

"That spark ignites a fire that burns inside me. I don't know why or how, but it blazes whenever I see you."

"Look, buddy, this is all very flattering. But I am simply not interested in you that way. I have a boyfriend." *You do?*

You're calling him your boyfriend right now? That's fast work. What if he tells other people? What if Eric finds out?

He shook his head emphatically. "That's not the kind of fire I'm talking about."

"Then what is it?"

"Part of me says it's hatred. I feel an intense hatred for you, and I am not sure why yet. There is a...supernatural sense to what is going on inside me."

He can say that again. Most things I feel are supernatural. Maybe that's why I'm so bothered by his presence on an emotional level. I definitely feel the same hatred.

"Now what?" Vickie asked.

"What do you mean?"

"I won't let you walk around here staring at me all day. You don't get to do that. You're creeping me out. Go do something else. Make some friends or... I don't know. I won't fight you. I doubt you would be able to handle me anyway."

He looked at her short stature, then laughed. "Whatever you say. But my senses do not lie. There is something here, and it is bad. We will have to find out eventually. And I will bet it will happen soon."

She rolled her eyes. "Whatever you say. But go home and stop stalking me."

Vickie turned to walk away again, but she could still feel his gaze boring into her back. Without looking, she knew he continued that unsettling, unnatural stare.

Why do I hate him too? Why would some random guy walk into this school and immediately establish himself as my enemy? What purpose does that serve?

"Is something bugging you?" Craig asked as she climbed into the SUV.

"I don't know. There's a new, weird guy in school here. I don't get it. He has a really odd vibe to him that makes me uncomfortable. And he seems infatuated with me."

He cocked an eyebrow. The word infatuated was not one he cared to hear even remotely connected to his girls.

"Don't worry about it, Dad. I don't really know what this is either. I can protect myself from him if I need to. But it's not the love kind of infatuation. It's…something else. I simply can't put my finger on it yet."

When they arrived home, Alexis stood in the kitchen with a huge smile on her face—the same smile she wore when she knew Eric would ask Vickie to Homecoming.

"What's going on? You look creepy." The vampire walked past her to take her things to her bedroom.

"I have a date for Homecoming." She practically shouted it from the rooftops.

"Are you serious?" Vickie squealed. The two girls hugged in excitement.

Her father, however, was less than thrilled. *You can't prevent her from growing up. But man, you are not ready for this.*

"I have a date. I have a date." She jumped up and down. "This is so great. Do you know what that means?"

Vickie nodded. "It means we can all go to the dance together."

"It'll be so much fun because we will have guys with us. Dance partners all night." She puffed her chest out and strutted across the kitchen floor.

"Okay, okay, so who is this guy and how ugly is he?" her father asked.

"Dad!" Alexis shot her an angry look. "He is not ugly. What, do you think I can only get ugly guys? Is that what you think of me?"

He laughed. "Oh, please. You know how beautiful you are. I'm sure the guys were simply too intimidated to ask you before now. One of them finally broke through and decided to give you a shot, eh?"

"Who is this guy?" Vickie asked. As soon as the words left her mouth, her stomach dropped again. *Oh no. Please, no. Anybody else.*

She already knew the answer.

"Will Rasch."

"Will Rasch? Are you kidding me?" Vickie froze in a combination of rage and fear.

"I know you have a hard time with him, but I've talked to him and he seems to be a really nice guy. Maybe you simply have to give him a chance."

Vickie stormed into her room and slammed the door shut.

After a beat of silence, Craig turned to his daughter. "Do you like this guy?"

"Oh, yes."

"Is he cute?"

"You know it."

"Do you trust him?"

"I...think so."

"Then that's all I need to hear. You've won me over. But now, you need to go into that bedroom and talk to her. She's obviously upset that you're dating this

Will guy, so see if you can get some answers from her."

Alexis knocked and stepped into Vickie's room. The vampire scrolled the Web mindlessly on her laptop with a scowl on her face.

"Can we talk?"

"What's there to talk about?" Vickie asked and waved her hand around. "I've told you how this guy gives me the creeps, that he gives me a scary impression, and that I think he's no good. And what do you do? You take him to Homecoming. And I have to be there to watch it."

"We don't know anything about this guy. It's an innocent date. It doesn't mean I'll date him forever. But he's cute, and he was really nice to me when he asked me out. Don't you think you can get through one night together without wanting to kill him?"

Vickie remained silent.

"Come on, Vickie. It's the first time a boy has asked me to a dance for real. This is my chance to enjoy some of the excitement you already have with Eric."

Oh, please, don't compare Will to Eric. That's an insult to Eric and any other decent boys out there who are simply looking for the right one. Will flat-out stated he hates me for no reason. That's who you want to date?

"I had planned to tell you about a conversation Will and I had tonight."

"Tonight?" Alexis looked at the clock. "He's not in any sports. What was he doing hanging around the school?"

"This was never answered. He merely stared at me in the hall."

"Did you confront him about it?"

"Of course. And you know what he said to me? He said he hates me. He can't explain why or how or what I did that would explain that, but he has a supernatural hatred toward me. I don't know what that means, either."

Alexis sat at the foot of her bed. "Maybe we can all get together and hash it out."

"No. It won't work, especially if there's a supernatural connection between the two of us. I don't know what the cause of it is. And more importantly, I need to find out what he plans to do about it or if he'll simply follow me around and hate me from a distance."

Her sister sighed. "Well, I need to be considerate about this, too. I don't want it to be torture for everybody involved, either."

The girls agreed to leave it there for now. That evening, they could both celebrate that they had dates for Homecoming. It was a big deal for each of them.

Vickie would experience her first date. Alexis would finally have a date for a dance. The two of them were growing up right before Craig's eyes. He sat in his recliner in the living room and stared out the living room window.

I'll need to keep an even closer eye on the two of them. I realized that maybe one of them would get a date soon and we could start going through that process. Now, I have to navigate it two at a time and with no Carol to help me. It's not fair, honey. Not fair at all. Anytime you want to come back and work with these girls, I am open for anything. Come back as a ghost, I don't care.

But come and help, because I'll be buried under teenaged girl hormones for the next few years, and I don't know what I'm doing.

CHAPTER THIRTY

Hannes sat in the pew of the cathedral, his gaze focused on the ornate architecture that covered every square inch of the historic building. He bowed his head and offered a prayer to the saints for protection and guidance.

He wasn't alone. Many others milled about in the cathedral. Some were tourists, snapping photos they weren't supposed to in the holy building. Others brought prayers and petitions or lit candles for their loved ones.

The moment was a necessary one for him to calm himself in preparation. He didn't have much time before he had to descend the steps into the crypt again for another meeting of the Slayer Circle. There had been discussion of a disturbance in the world, and he wanted to bring those petitions to the saints directly in hopes that they would be successful in ridding the world of evil.

He walked over to the candles and lit one in prayer. Fear welled in the pit of his stomach when he thought about why they were meeting that evening.

A few men in the Circle had spread rumors among their members that there was a real vampire out there. He didn't know the details yet, but he intended to find out when the emergency meeting began. *All I need to know is that they think there are vampires out there again. We need to take every precaution possible to stop this from turning into a worldwide disaster. Not again. No man will have to sacrifice his children again to the bloodthirsty species.*

The Circle had always dedicated itself to the cause of combating the vampire race, to their supposed success. To hear that there were surviving vampires was a slap in the face to every member of the Circle, past or present. If untrue, claiming that vampires survived was tremendously disrespectful, as the group was taught to honor those who fought in the Sang Crusades and sacrificed their lives to save humanity from the curse of these unnatural creatures.

So when the old man had stepped forward with his fire and brimstone presentation, many stood in awe of the concerns he had raised. If untrue, he was either crazy or a pitiful liar.

If true, the work of the Sang Crusades was a failure and a new war would be waged.

Now, the Circle had decisions to make, and Hannes needed to be there.

He stood and made his way to the stairs leading to the basement crypt of the cathedral. Again, he pulled the hood of his black robe over his head as he walked down the stairs until he was surrounded by other robe-clad figures.

A loud gong was struck, ear-piercing in the confines of the underground space.

"We have heeded the warning." Gabriel, the leader of the Circle, stepped forward and stood behind a small wooden podium. "When Jannik's messenger came to us, sadly, we didn't give him the proper respect he deserved. I have seen to it that new research is conducted. As we speak, the claims are under investigation. We cannot be careless in our work. If indeed his vision is true, it means the Circle did not finish their task four hundred years ago, and we need to step forward and put an end to it right now." He pounded his fist on the podium. "It is our only task and we are failing."

A hand raised. "Brothers of the Slayer Circle, my name is Gregor, and I have successfully been able to unearth more information that could lead us to the alleged survivor —and possibly others."

He unfolded a piece of paper with a few notes scribbled on them. "There is one on the Internet who claims to be a survivor. This is not simply someone who says he or she is a vampire. There are many of those. Her claims appear to be genuine, and she speaks of coming from here in Austria. The name she uses is VickieVampire, and we have traced her to Wisconsin."

"Excellent work, Gregor," Gabriel said approvingly. "I must also warn you all that I feel a strong disturbance in my soul that I cannot shake. Something bigger is happening. It is bigger than simply the last vampire surviving the Crusades. I worry—deep down in my soul—that there are others."

"Other vampires?" a voice asked.

"No. But I don't know what they are. It's possible that

the Sang Crusade also missed other breeds of supernatural creatures. For example, we have only recently discovered that vampires and Sanguinarians are two completely different beasts.

"And unfortunately, it is possible that the Sangs as a race have survived as well. If that is the case, we must prepare to hunt these creatures and finish the work our forefathers started."

A nervous cheer erupted among the crowd of worshippers. This was heavy information they had to process and the first time in their lives they had heard any news quite like this.

And now, they would have to find VickieVampire and any other supernatural beings connected to her.

"They are out there, my brothers," Gabriel said. "Of this I am sure. And they are vulnerable to attack, so we must act quickly."

***

Vickie sat up in her bed and snapped instantly awake to unleash a loud gasp. She clutched her chest and stomach and clawed at the tightness in her body.

This has never felt so severe before. What is wrong? Am I going to die? Am I dying right now?

She leapt out of bed and charged into the hallway. Alexis stumbled out of her room, her expression both bewildered and concerned.

"Is everything okay?" she whispered in an effort to not wake her father in the next room.

Vickie's chest heaved as she practically hyperventilated. Her fingernails dragged across her chest and stomach. To Alexis, it looked like she was trying to dig into her midsection.

"Stop. You'll hurt yourself."

Before she could reach her friend, the girl ran through the kitchen. Without unlocking the side door, she yanked on it and shattered the wood frame with her powerful grip. Vickie ran out into the driveway where she paced feverishly while tears streamed down her face.

"Vickie. Vickie, stop! You're okay. Nothing is happening."

Her words seemed to fall on deaf ears. Alexis grabbed her and wrapped her arms tightly around her. "Calm down. Control your breathing. You're safe here. You're safe." *Please don't accidentally crush me to death for trying to help.*

Alexis looked at the door where her father now stood in his pajamas, a befuddled look on his face. "What just—"

"I don't know, Dad. Vickie's freaking out about something and I can't figure out what."

He surveyed the damage to the door, shook his head, and sighed at the new project his adopted daughter had unwittingly created for him.

But of greater concern to both of them was the panicked girl who trembled with fear in the driveway.

"Something bad…something bad…something bad…" She continued to repeat those words over and over again while Alexis held her as tightly as she could in a futile effort to calm her.

The adventures and challenges don't end here. Follow Vicki, Alexis and Craig as she continues her journey as a teenage vampire in The Girl With A Secret.

The adventures and challenges don't end here. Follow Vicki, Alexis and Craig as she continues her journey as a teenage vampire in The Girl With A Secret.

AVAILABLE FOR PURCHASE HERE

AUTHOR NOTES - MARTHA CARR

MAY 29, 2019

It's been an interesting month with an unexpected gift. Sometimes, if we're willing, when a hard thing happens in a life, when the initial shock wears off, we can make an interesting choice. We can ask, how can I honor what happened here? I'll start with the gift, first because those who know me (like a lot of you readers), know I like to be helpful, reach out, show up, listen. But I'm not always as good at being the vulnerable one. This part of the story – what I did with the gift – is teaching me that from pain can also come opportunity, joy, new growth.

This part of the story started in the middle of the night just two weeks ago. I went to bed just fine and woke up around two a.m. with a sharp pain right in the middle of my chest. Not sharp enough to call an ambulance, but bad enough to keep me awake and wonder... Is this ER worthy?

Normally, I like to wait and see if things go away on their own. I already spend enough time hanging around hospitals and doctors. It comes from having cancer seven times and routinely getting poked and scanned and drinking something weird that glows iridescent blue. I like to wait and see if things will go away by themselves.

But...

My big sister, Diana, passed away last October and in her final weeks she was deteriorating rapidly, but wouldn't call anyone for help and told no one. She was a well-respected surgeon and must have known things weren't going well. I even spoke to her and sensed something wasn't quite right. I asked if I could help, even pressed a little – but she said she was fine. A month later she was gone.

When she died, I promised myself in honor of this funny, clever woman who was constantly treating patients who couldn't pay, (and who came to her funeral in droves), and could fly her own plane, and embroider amazing things that I would not only ask for help, I'd take it.

So that night I got up and went to the ER where they immediately thought heart attack, tested me and said "Not a heart attack." The resident said, "Maybe it's an ulcer or stress or anxiety," and sent me home without any further tests. Whatever.

The pain was still there six hours later. I thought of Diana and tried again. I made a promise. I also picked a different ER and this time they did a CT scan. Turns out I needed an emergency appendectomy and one hour later, I was down one organ. But, since I kept going back when it really seemed like it might be nothing, it was relatively simple. Waiting could have made it life threatening.

When my friend, Lou Ann who dances easily with strangers and laughs at everything and is always willing to go try something new figured out where I was, she asked what room number and was on her way. I didn't protest and instead, welcomed in the company. She stayed well past midnight, chatting with the Offspring and asking him about music, keeping him distracted.

Let's go back to the gift. What I'm learning is everything is easier when done as a group where we give some and we take some. Like a seesaw in action. The bar is no longer, if I can do it I will and instead has changed to, what do I want to do, and what would this be like with others?

New opportunities are showing up and great things are underway. One of them is a new series, The Peabrain Adventures about the magic inside all of us and in it is a sister named, Diana who's a surgeon so that for a little while, I can visit with her again and create a few last adventures. More adventures to follow.

AUTHOR NOTES - MICHAEL ANDERLE

JUNE 3, 2019

THANK YOU for not only reading this story but these *Author Notes* as well.

(I think I've been good with always opening with "thank you." If not, I need to edit the other *Author Notes*!)

RANDOM (*sometimes*) THOUGHTS?

When we write stories, we often use concepts that many of us share (like going to school.)

For many readers, high school was a good time. For others, not so much. I personally had an 'ok' time in high school. I got through it, and I'm not traumatized.

I consider that a win.

However, it doesn't stop me from wondering at times what I would do differently if I was back in school. Would I study more? Would I start a business like I have now and plan for the future, or would I perhaps do stupid stuff that I never did the first time through high school?

This presumes that I remember what I know now. If you told me I had to go back to school and I wouldn't remember anything of the future I'd flat turn you down. There is no way I wish to go back to high school ignorant again.

So, we tell stories about Vampires that have to deal with high school so we don't have to.

I hope you enjoy them ;-)

AROUND THE WORLD IN 80 DAYS

One of the interesting (at least to me) aspects of my life is the ability to work from anywhere and at any time. In the future, I hope to re-read my own *Author Notes* and remember my life as a diary entry.

Cave in the Sky(™), Las Vegas Nv USA

The time is 8:27 AM in the morning, I've been up for three (3) hours and I am already mainlining Coca-cola.

It's all for the caffeine.

I've written one blurb for a book (Chuck Dixon's) coming out Thursday and an author note for the Alison Brownstone book coming out Wednesday.

In an hour, I have an art meeting for the Opus X project coming out (most likely) November 2nd / 3rd on the 4th anniversary of Death Becomes Her - The Kurtherian Gambit book 01.

The book that started all of this (for me).

I wouldn't be in this place, typing these author notes right now if it wasn't for you who read our stories, share them with friends, and let us know you love the characters.

So, a few months early I wish to say 'thank you' for all that you do, and for all of our LMBPN books you've read.

You change lives.

Including mine.

FAN PRICING

$0.99 Saturdays (new LMBPN stuff) and $0.99 Wednesday (both LMBPN books and friends of LMBPN books.) Get great stuff from us and others at tantalizing prices.

Go ahead, I bet you can't read just one.

Sign up here: http://lmbpn.com/email/.

HOW TO MARKET FOR BOOKS YOU LOVE

Review them so others have your thoughts, tell friends and the dogs of your enemies (because who wants to talk with enemies?)... *Enough said ;-)*

Ad Aeternitatem,

Michael Anderle

<u>JOIN THE ORICERAN UNIVERSE FAN GROUP ON FACEBOOK!</u>